AUTOCORRECT

Also by Etgar Keret

Fly Already

The Seven Good Years

Suddenly, a Knock on the Door

The Girl on the Fridge

The Nimrod Flipout

*The Bus Driver Who Wanted
to Be God & Other Stories*

AUTOCORRECT

[*STORIES*]

ETGAR KERET

Translated by
Jessica Cohen and
Sondra Silverston

RIVERHEAD BOOKS · NEW YORK · 2025

RIVERHEAD BOOKS
An imprint of Penguin Random House LLC
1745 Broadway, New York, NY 10019
penguinrandomhouse.com

Previous publication information for these short stories may be found on page 197.

Book design by Christina Nguyen

Library of Congress Cataloging-in-Publication Data

Names: Keret, Etgar, 1967– author. | Silverston, Sondra, translator. |
Cohen, Jessica, translator.
Title: Autocorrect : stories / Etgar Keret ; translated by
Jessica Cohen and Sondra Silverston.
Other titles: Oṭoḳoreḳṭ. English
Description: New York : Riverhead Books, 2025.
Identifiers: LCCN 2024042008 (print) | LCCN 2024042009 (ebook) |
ISBN 9780593717233 (hardcover) | ISBN 9780593717257 (ebook)
Subjects: LCGFT: Short stories.
Classification: LCC PJ5054.K375 O8613 2025 (print) |
LCC PJ5054.K375 (ebook) | DDC [Fic]—dc23
LC record available at https://lccn.loc.gov/2024042008
LC ebook record available at https://lccn.loc.gov/2024042009

An earlier version of this collection first published in Israel as אתגר קרת in
different form by Kinneret Zmora-Bitan Dvir, Shoham, in 2024.
First English-language collection published by Riverhead, 2025.

Printed in the United States of America
1st Printing

The authorized representative in the EU for product safety and compliance is
Penguin Random House Ireland, Morrison Chambers, 32 Nassau Street,
Dublin D02 YH68, Ireland, https://eu-contact.penguin.ie.

For Hamutal

CONTENTS

A World Without Selfie Sticks · 1

Gondola · 11

Point of No Return · 23

Mesopotamian Hell · 29

Mitzvah · 31

Modern Dance · 41

Soulo · 45

Good as New · 51

Genesis, Chapter 0 · 57

Eating Olives at the End of the World · 63

Strong Opinions on Burning Issues · 65

Autocorrect · 71

The Future Is Not What It Used to Be · 79

Guided Tour · 83

Outside · 87

A Dog for a Dog · 91

Present Perfect · 101

Director's Cut · 107

Gravity · 109

Chinese Singles Day · 115

Insomnia · 119

Zen for Beginners · 121

Squirrels · 125

Life: Spoiler Alert · 133

A Hypothetical Question · 135

Cherry Garcia Memories with M&M's on Top · 141

Lucky Us · 147

Earthquake · 151

Undo · 161

Corners · 167

For the Woman Who Has Everything · 173

Intention · 183

Polar Bear · 191

AUTOCORRECT

A WORLD WITHOUT
SELFIE STICKS

n retrospect, I shouldn't have yelled at Not-Debbie. Debbie herself always said that yelling doesn't solve anything. But what is a person supposed to do when, a week after saying a tearful goodbye at the airport to his girlfriend, who was flying to Australia to do her doctorate, he bumps into her at an East Village Starbucks?

When I saw her in the coffee shop, harassing the barista with questions about their milk substitutes, and I asked her how she could come back to New York without even letting me know, she just gave me a cold look and said impatiently, "Mister, I don't know who you are. You must have me mixed up with someone else." That's when I lost it. After almost three years together, I'd hoped for more civil treatment. So when she said she didn't know me, instead of arguing, I stood in the middle of Starbucks and yelled out all the intimate details I knew about her, including the scar on her back from when she fell on our trip to Yosemite and the hairy mole in her left armpit. Not-Debbie didn't reply, just gave me a shocked look as two café employees pushed me out.

I sat down on a bench in the street and started to cry. Five weeks earlier, when Debbie told me she was moving to Australia, I'd been devastated, but I understood that the split was inevitable: the University of Sydney had offered her a doctoral grant, and I'd just been appointed to head a team at one of the hottest big-data start-ups in the country. And, honestly, though the separation was painful, it wasn't cruel or humiliating, like that frigid encounter in Starbucks.

Suddenly, I felt a gentle touch on my shoulder, and when I looked up, I saw Not-Debbie standing next to me. "Let's be clear," she whispered, "I might look like her, with the mole and all, but I'm not her. Really!"

Not-Debbie and I moved to another café on Third Avenue. She ordered a weak cappuccino with a lot of foam, just like Debbie used to, gave me a searching look, also familiar to me, and began telling me the craziest story I'd ever heard. It seemed that Not-Debbie was also named Deborah, but she hadn't come to New York that morning from Australia. She'd come from a parallel world. I'm not kidding—that's what she said between sips of her weak cappuccino. She wasn't part of an alien invasion or the result of a scientific military experiment gone wrong. She was here as a contestant on a TV game show called *Vive la Différence*, the top-rated program in the alternate universe she came from.

Five participants in the show are sent to a universe that contains everything they have in their own world, except for one thing, and that's what it's all about—figuring out that one thing that exists in their world but not in the one they've been sent to. The contestants are filmed 24/7, each on their own special channel, and the first one to discover what that missing item is and say it aloud is instantly returned to the TV studio in the world they came from, to the cheers of the audience and a million-dollar prize. And, to raise the stakes, while the winner celebrates, the rest of the contestants have to live the rest of their lives in the alternate universe they've been sent to, never really knowing if they've lost the game or if it's still on. This sounded to me like a hell of a price to pay for the losers, but Not-Debbie said it didn't bother her at all, because her ex was a real asshole and she hadn't spoken to her parents for years.

It all felt too incredible to be a lie, and Not-Debbie spoke with such sincerity that I just had to believe it. Last season's winner, she said, was an immigrant from Ghana who discovered that the missing item in the alternate world the contestants had been sent to was a selfie stick.

"A fucking selfie stick, can you believe it?" Not-Debbie said. "I would have never figured it out."

I asked her a few more questions. It turned out that, like Debbie, Not-Debbie had studied clinical psychology, but she wasn't interested in being a therapist or getting a doctorate, which is why she now found herself stuck in an administrative job at some rich college in upstate New York. I told her about my split from Debbie. About how I'd gone to the airport with her the week before and hadn't left the terminal until I saw her plane take off for Australia. She nodded and said it made sense. Contestants are never sent to the hemisphere where their parallels live, and if Debbie hadn't flown to Sydney, then she would probably have ended up in Buenos Aires or Auckland. "I'm glad she left," she said, giving me the smile that had made me fall in love with Debbie two and a half years before. "With all due respect to Auckland, nothing beats New York."

When we finished our coffee, Not-Debbie insisted on paying, and right before we were about to go our separate ways, I offered to help her win the prize on the show. In order to find what her world had that ours didn't, Not-Debbie had to be exposed to as much information as possible as quickly as possible, and I, as a computer person with expertise in databases, could help. When I saw her hesitate, I quickly backtracked and said that if helping her or using computers were against the rules, then . . . But Not-Debbie smiled and interrupted me.

"It's not that," she said. "I just don't want to drag you into this whole complicated business. It's not like I'm just a girl you never met before."

I explained that there was nothing complicated about it. Even though I'd been with Debbie for two and a half years, she was Not-Debbie and we'd just met today, and if it was okay, I'd be glad to help her look for the missing thing. And who knows, maybe in the process, I'd become a TV star in an alternate universe.

At four in the morning, after nine straight hours of searching the technological, geographic, and culinary databases (would you believe that, in the show's first season, the parallel world was a world without maple syrup?), Not-Debbie said she couldn't keep her eyes open anymore. I changed the sheets on the bed in my small studio apartment for her and she fell asleep instantly. I sat and watched Not-Debbie sleep. It was weird, but I felt that, in those nine hours, I'd learned more about her than I'd ever known about my Debbie in the entire two and something years we'd lived together. The possibilities she raised in our search for the missing element revealed so much about her dreams, her desires, her fears. It wasn't that she didn't resemble Debbie, but there was something else about her: she was open, brave, mesmerizing, and wild. I don't really know what to call it when it happens with someone who is both your ex and someone you've never met, but I fell in love. And while Not-Debbie slept in my apartment, so close that I could smell her shampoo, I pictured the other four contestants on the show still searching for flying cats, electric ear cleaners, eyebrow deodorants, or whatever it was that was missing in this imperfect world. And I knew that all it took for Not-Debbie to stay here with me forever was for one of them to find it. I closed my eyes.

When Not-Debbie woke me at one in the afternoon, she seemed a little slower. She told me it had taken an average of fifteen hours for the winners of previous seasons to find the missing element, and she'd been searching for more than a day already. "That's it," she said, "one of the others must have found it by now."

I tried to reassure her. After all, there was no way of knowing—maybe they were baffled, wandering around Manhattan or wherever they'd been sent, and she could still win. "Maybe," Not-Debbie said, suddenly smiling, "but the truth is that from the minute I went on the show, I've been fantasizing about losing and starting a new life in this world—a better, less painful life than the one I had back home."

I didn't say anything, and she looked at me softly, unlike the way Debbie had ever looked at me. "Honestly," she said, and touched my face with the back of her hand, "who cares what's missing in this world? You're here."

In bed, when I asked her if she was on birth control, she shook her head and said with a smile she really hoped that, of all the possible parallel worlds, she hadn't landed in one without condoms. It was a joke, but when she said it, I could see her hesitate a second out of fear that maybe it was actually true and that saying it aloud would return her to her world and separate us forever. After the sex, when I suggested that we check out the astronomy, geopolitics, and history data-bases, she said she'd rather have sex again.

Later, we went out for a walk in Central Park and ate hot dogs. Not-Debbie told me that in her world, she's a vegetarian for reasons of conscience, but she feels that here in this world, which isn't her own, it's okay for her to eat a hot dog. "I don't want to win," she said as we stood by the lake, "I don't want to go back. I want to be here, with you." We spent the rest of the day in the city, showing each other our favorite places in Manhattan.

That's how we arrived at Trinity Church. It was already evening and the illuminated church looked enchanted, more like a palace in a Disney movie than a real place. I told her that I'd happened to walk past it ten years ago, when I'd just arrived in the city, and I swore that if I ever got married, I'd do it there. Not-Debbie laughed and said being sure about the church was good, now all I had to do was find a girl who'd agree to marry me in it. I smiled, too, and right after we kissed, Not-Debbie said, "Let's go inside, I'm dying to see the place where we're getting married."

The church was fairly empty, and from the minute we walked in, Not-Debbie kept looking around uneasily, as if she were searching for something. I asked her if everything was all right, and she said yes, she was just looking for something. When I asked her what, she looked at me as if I were an idiot and said, "God." Then she added, "This is a church, right?" I nodded, and she said, "So He'll probably be back in a minute." I tried to calm her down. I said that I personally didn't believe in God, but even the people who do say you can't see Him.

Not-Debbie shook her head slowly. "Wow, that's it! In your world, there are churches and mosques and synagogues, exactly like in mine, only there's not really a God in them. Don't you get it? It's a world without Go—" She didn't manage to finish that sentence, at least not in my world.

Six years have passed since then, and I still try to imagine what happened to Not-Debbie, how she arrived at the flashy studio and was welcomed with cheers from the audience and compliments from a pair of sleek presenters, who told her she had won a million dollars. Sometimes when I imagine it, she's happy and tears of joy run down her face, but most of the time, she's sad, searching the studio, looking for and not finding me. My heart might want to picture her happy, but my ego—my ego insists on believing that the day we spent together was as meaningful to her as it was to me. Less than a year after she slipped through my fingers, I married Debbie in Trinity Church. Life in Sydney wasn't for her, and two months after she returned to the city, we made a spur-of-the-moment decision to get married. Sex with her, by the way, is never as spectacular as it was with Not-Debbie, but it's pleasant enough and familiar, and we have two adorable children, Zack and Deborah Junior, who will have to learn to live, as we did, in a godless world.

GONDOLA

His Tinder profile said his name was Oshik, he was thirty-eight, married with no kids, looking for a serious relationship. Dorit, who wasn't new to online dating, had never come across such an unusual line, and he sounded so square and had such high cheekbones and enormous blue eyes that she was curious enough to give it a try.

The only other Oshik she'd ever known was her dad's uncle, an insurance broker from Netanya, and he was eaten by a shark. It was a big story back in the day, and there was an intimidating TV reporter at the shiva, who pounced on Dorit and her older sister, Rotem, demanding to interview them. Rotem told her that Oshik was an angel now, and that they would remember him forever. When the reporter asked Dorit what she would recall about Uncle Oshik in twenty years, Dorit stammered that the thing she would always remember was that a shark had eaten him.

Oshik suggested they meet at five p.m. at a branch of Roladin. Dorit was used to men on Tinder asking to meet at her apartment—they'd have had their first date in her bedroom if they could—but this guy not only wanted an afternoon meeting at a café frequented by everyone's grandma, he also said he'd have to leave after an hour because he and his wife were going to a wedding out of town.

They sat facing each other, sipping coffee. Dorit wondered how long it would take to get to the punch line, but Oshik was in no hurry. She sensed that he was attracted to her and that he was a little embarrassed by it. His questions were stodgy: What was her childhood like? What were her greatest fears? What music did she listen to on Friday afternoons when everything was slowing down for Shabbat? The vibe was more like an arranged-marriage date than a Tinder hookup. It was weird, and in some way she couldn't explain, she liked the weirdness. She found it much more appealing to tell Oshik about how her sister had taught her to do a cartwheel when they were kids than to share her feelings on anal sex with a tattooed hipster she'd swiped right on five minutes ago. And this Oshik guy was really interested in her. More than interested: he fell in love. Dorit, who was thirty-two and had finally broken up with an egotistical tech bro who saw the world and her as algorithms to be optimized, felt that this was the perfect time for a guy called Oshik who was gentle and romantic. Gentle, romantic, and married.

The screen saver on his phone was a picture of him and his wife in a gondola. When Dorit asked, Oshik mumbled that it was an old picture from a trip to Venice, and quickly changed the subject. Dorit took a picture of the screen saver when Oshik went to the bathroom, and later, at home, she examined it closely. Oshik's wife was pretty. Prettier than her. She had golden-brown curls, a long neck, and a smooth, radiant complexion that seemed unblemished no matter how much Dorit enlarged the photo. The wife's smile showed off her glistening white teeth, and she wore an expensive-looking wedding ring. Oshik looked contemplative, and there was no ring on his finger. He hadn't worn one on their date, either. In the gondola picture, his left arm rested on his wife's shoulder, but there was nothing sexy or charged about the touch. It looked more like a hug you'd give your army buddy than a romantic embrace.

Their second date was also at Roladin. Dorit wanted to pay this time, but Oshik wouldn't hear of it. He ordered a cinnamon roll and told her that when he was a soldier, every time he got in trouble and was confined to barracks, he would go to the canteen and console himself with a cinnamon roll. Dorit asked if that happened a lot, and he nodded and said almost proudly that he was probably the worst soldier in the history of the IDF.

They had a really good talk, and afterward, Oshik suggested they go to her place. He tried to make it sound like the most casual thing in the world, but Dorit picked up on his anxiety. She said he was cute and she'd be happy to have him over, but before anything started up she had to understand the situation with his wife. There were lots of married guys on Tinder, but Oshik was the first one she'd seen who said he was looking for something serious. "What exactly does that mean?" she asked, grinning. "How serious can it be if you're married?"

Oshik nodded. "When you put it that way, it does sound dumb," he said. She asked if his wife knew he was seeing her, and he stammered and said she didn't, but they weren't sleeping together anyway; they were more like friends. "I really am looking for a serious relationship!" he said, and stroked Dorit's hand hesitantly. "But I also know that I'll probably never leave her, and it's important for me to put that on the table. Love me, love my dog, as the saying goes." Dorit smiled and said she was actually quite fond of dogs, and that she didn't know anyone other than her grandfather who still used that expression.

Sex with Oshik reminded her of sex in high school. In a good way. Everything was almost childishly exciting. He caressed, kissed, and licked every part of her body, and looked happy and grateful the whole time. Dorit closed her eyes and thought about a million things, including the Gondola, which was what she'd started privately calling his wife. She felt no guilt. Oshik's body showed her how hungry he was for touch, and if he wasn't getting it at home, she saw no reason why he shouldn't get it with her. Especially if, while they were at it, he was going to keep making her feel like the hottest woman in the world.

At the beginning, Dorit thought of it as a fling. A sort of eccentric episode in her rather conventional life. An amusing anecdote she'd be able to tell one day, about how she dated a married guy who got excited every time they kissed and showed up to their dates with cinnamon rolls, Cornettos, and pudding cups. Oshik may not have been the most articulate person Dorit had ever met, but he was kind and funny and curious, and he loved her so much that some of the love rubbed off on her. Also, they talked about everything. Everything except his wife. When she tried asking about her, Oshik said that when he and Dorit slept together, he didn't feel like he was cheating, but when they talked about his wife, he did. That's why he wouldn't even say her name. "I don't tell her anything about you, either," he quipped, but Dorit didn't crack a smile. She told Oshik that the mistress thing had worked for her at first: living in the moment, no expectations. But now that a year had passed, it wasn't enough. She wanted more: to live together, to have a child—not now, but one day—and to go to her parents for holiday dinners. If his relationship with the Gondola was really so friendly, surely she'd understand and let him go?

Oshik gazed at Dorit with his giant blue eyes, on the verge of tears. "Are you saying you want to break up because I don't spend the Passover seder with your folks?" he asked. "Matza ball soup and Uncle Morris's lame jokes, that's what we're lacking?"

"Yes," Dorit said. "What can I say: of all the girls in the world, you landed on the one weirdo who likes her men unmarried."

"It's not fair," he whispered. "I told you from the beginning—"

"Yes," Dorit interrupted, "you told me I had to love your dog. And back then, it sounded fine. But now we've reached the point where you have to choose: it's me or the dog."

If it had been up to Dorit, that's where it would have ended. But Oshik pleaded. He said she was right, it was all true, but things were complicated and he needed time. He didn't tell her what he needed time for—to prepare the Gondola for a separation or to decide whom he was choosing. Either way, Dorit told Oshik he would have to make up his mind by the last day of Hanukkah.

———

After that talk, something between them soured. They didn't
fight or hurl insults, but they grew distant, unnecessarily cau-
tious, thinking twice before they shared a thought or a feeling. They saw each other less, and when they did, Dorit's
ultimatum hovered over them like a curse. Deep in her heart,
she knew Oshik wouldn't leave the Gondola. And even deeper
in that same heart, she knew it would be very hard for her to
give him up.

Once, when they'd gone to the beach, Oshik had shown her
the tall, ugly, marble-coated apartment building where he
lived, and on the morning of the first day of Hanukkah, Dorit
found herself sitting on a bench across the street from the
building. She didn't have much of a plan. On the way there,
she'd told herself that she just wanted to see Oshik and his
wife walking down the street together so that she could understand where she stood. But after waiting on the bench for
almost an hour, she was also able to picture the Gondola coming home with her shopping, and herself walking over to talk
to her—not to snitch or harass her, just to make a connection,
and then the two of them would arrange to meet without Oshik's even knowing. After another twenty minutes on the
bench, Dorit could imagine herself confronting Oshik and

the Gondola right there in the middle of the street, making a scene and embarrassing him. Embarrassing herself. This thought frightened her, and she got up and took the bus home.

The next time she saw Oshik, after they had sex she asked him to tell her the Gondola's name. "Yardena," Oshik said, and pressed his face into the pillow. "Yardena, Ruth, Greta Garbo. What difference does it make?"

The following morning, Dorit went back to the ugly marble building. She bought herself a jelly doughnut and sat down to eat it on the bench. She ate the doughnut as slowly as humanly possible, taking tiny little bites, licking the jelly. It took almost half an hour, but there was still no sign of Oshik or the Gondola. Eventually, a young woman with a feather tattooed on her neck came out of the building holding a cigarette and sat down next to Dorit to smoke. Dorit asked her for a cigarette. She didn't really smoke, but she felt that it would buy her a few more minutes to wait there without feeling pathetic. While they smoked together, the Feather started talking. She said her name was Lianne and she was studying occupational therapy and worked as a doorwoman at the building across the street. The people who lived there, she told Dorit, were filthy rich, but nice. At least some of them were. This week a whole bunch of them had given her envelopes with Hanukkah cards and cash, like a holiday bonus, and the old lady from the penthouse had handed her a hundred-dollar bill. She hadn't made that kind of money even at her bat mitzvah. She asked Dorit if she worked in the area, and Dorit, who did not usually lie, said she was a dental hygienist at a clinic nearby. After a few seconds, she added that she was pretty sure two of her clients lived in that building. Their names were Oshik and . . . the wife's name had slipped her mind, but their last name was Arbel and they were really nice.

"Oshik Arbel?" the Feather said. "I know him. He's kind of weird but he is a sweetheart."

"Yeah. I clean his teeth, and his wife's."

"Are you sure? I know Arbel, he's not married. He's one of those loner types."

When Dorit pulled out her phone and held up the picture of Oshik with the Gondola, the Feather smiled and said, "Oh, that's Yardena. She's his sister. She lives in Berlin, but she and her husband visit all the time."

On the seventh day of Hanukkah, Oshik called and jokingly suggested they go out to celebrate the evening before her ultimatum expired. But when Dorit said she wasn't in the mood, he backed off and said he'd come over and they could order in. They both knew this was probably going to be their last night together, and it was better to have a sad breakup at home, without an audience. Oshik arrived with a box of candy he'd been given by a client from Nazareth. They kissed and caressed as if everything were normal, and Dorit tried to be detached. She'd thought it was going to be hard, that she'd feel angry and distant, but even now that she knew he'd lied to her for a whole year, it felt like the most natural thing when he kissed her. If it had been the other way around—if she'd discovered that the man she was seeing was secretly married—she wouldn't have been able to forgive hm. But there was something about Oshik's lie that, although annoying, didn't really make her angry. He must have genuinely loved her, and only her, but at the same time he was afraid that without an imaginary gondola sailing across the horizon, they would be in each other's lives 24-7, each taking ownership of the other's soul.

The Thai food was slightly cold. "Here," Oshik said, switching their dishes, "mine's actually okay. Not piping hot, but warm. It's good, right?" Dorit ate in silence, and Oshik also said nothing as he chewed Dorit's cold noodles. When they'd finished, he murmured, "I love you. I love you more than anything. More than her, more than me, more than those cinnamon rolls in the army. Do you believe me?" Dorit wanted to lash out at him, to tell him she knew everything, he could stop the act. But she only nodded. "If this is our last time together," Oshik added, "then I'd rather we not sleep together. I know breakup sex is a thing, but I can't take it." Dorit still said nothing. "Okay," Oshik said. "I guess I'd better go." But instead of getting up, he stayed slumped on Dorit's old armchair, and after a few minutes he started crying.

His tears were real. The pain, everything was real, everything except the stupid story about his wife. She went over to him, sat on his lap, and kissed him.

"If this is our last time," he said again, "I'd rather not . . ."

"It's not," she said. "It's not."

After the sex, she told him she was willing to keep their arrangement, but she wanted a child. "You and the Gondola are never going to have a baby. Don't you want to be a father?"

Oshik shrugged and said he never really had—he didn't like himself enough. But now that he pictured a child who was half-Dorit, it suddenly sounded like a pretty good idea.

For Nur's third birthday, the three of them went to Italy. Oshik's wife was in Boston for work, and he suggested they sneak in their own overseas trip. In Verona, they saw the famous Romeo and Juliet balcony. Near Milan, they visited a lovely amusement park full of unicorns and fairies. And in Venice, of course, they took a gondola ride. Nur was overjoyed. She kept laughing and trying to jump into the water. Oshik and Dorit had to physically restrain her. "You little fishy," Oshik said, mussing Nur's hair as she wriggled on his lap. He pulled out his phone. "Before you go disappearing into the canal," he said, "let's get a picture of you and Mom and me in the gondola, okay?" Nur pouted and shook her head. Oshik smiled. "It's fine," he said, putting the phone back in his pocket. "We don't have to."

POINT OF NO RETURN

Not five minutes after I get off the Zoom call with management, Rinat comes over and says she wants to talk. I tell her sure. It's good to talk. I'm still on an adrenaline rush from the call. I was very tentative when I started my presentation, but I aced it—even Chemi was supportive and said that as far as he was concerned, we were good to go.

Rinat and I sit down in the kitchen. We usually have these talks in the living room, but the cleaner is here today and he's mopping the floors. Rinat gives me a sad look, which I find somewhat reassuring. If it had been an angry look, I would have known I was about to get raked over the coals, but a sad look could just be a fight with one of her sanctimonious sisters or a fender bender. "Okay," I say, in my most accepting voice. "What did you want to talk about?" I'm a little hurt that she didn't ask how my presentation went. She knows I've been preparing it for two weeks. But I don't want to fight, I just want to get through this conversation, listen to her tell me that her naturopath sister says we're too materialistic, and then we'll move on. But she sits quietly for a moment and then she says she wants Nigel to be part of the conversation. I tell her fine. My attitude is: I'm going to agree with anything she says. Although it does seem a little weird that she wants our Nigerian cleaner to join in.

Nigel sits down at the table, withdrawn. He doesn't look at me, only at Rinat and the floor. Rinat informs me that she and Nigel are in love. She says it's been going on for a long time but they just didn't know how to tell me. They both feel that their love, which fills their world with light, is cruel and unfair toward me, but they can no longer deny it.

"Rinat," I say, "are you out of your fucking mind?"

"Hey!" Nigel says, intervening for the first time. "Do not curse at her!"

"You keep your mouth shut!" I snap at Nigel. "If you know what's good for you, you'll stay out of this."

Rinat raises her voice: "Yair! You will not speak to him like that, d'you hear me?"

"Like what? What's wrong with how I'm speaking?"

"You're talking to him like . . ." She chokes up. "Like he's some slave you can order around—"

"Stop it!" I interrupt. "Don't make me out like some kind of racist. I'm talking to him like he's a guy who's fucking my wife."

"No, you are not," Nigel butts in again. "You are speaking to me like you are my master. It is not my fault that you are a shitty husband."

I've had enough. I hit the pause button. That's the nice thing about simulated life: it's just like life, except you can always stop, change a few parameters, and recalibrate. When I created Rinat, I wanted her to be flirty, to make me a little jealous. It never occurred to me that she'd end up having an affair with the cleaner. So, for starters, I increase her monogamy factor, and to be on the safe side I also give Nigel a lazy eye and take his intelligence down a couple of notches.

The system takes about half an hour to reboot, so I get up to go find something to snack on. In the kitchen, I run into Dikla, who's taking a break from her own simulation to make a sandwich. She makes one for me, too. When I tell her about what happened with Nigel, she bursts out laughing. "That is *so* you," she says. "Your wife cheats on you with the cleaner right under your nose, and you don't even notice."

"Hey, did you ever cheat on me?" I ask her. "I mean, not with someone in your simulation—with someone in life."

Dikla shakes her head and keeps grinning. "Even if you did," I add, "I'm totally cool with it, honestly."

"Oh, really?" Dikla gives me an amused look. "You're so cool with it that you almost cracked your poor cleaner's head open?"

"In the simulation," I point out. "In real life, you know I'm chill. Have you ever seen me—"

"With Avri," she cuts in. "When you went to take care of your mom. But after she died, I felt guilty and we stopped right away."

I stand there frozen, facing Dikla, with a salami-and-mustard sandwich in my right hand and a kitchen knife in my left. Neither of us says anything.

Finally, I say, "It's lucky my mom died, then. And thank you for not fucking Avri anymore because you felt sorry for an orphan."

"I knew it," Dikla mutters. "I knew you'd be a baby about this . . ."

"You knew it," I say coldly, "and yet you told me. And now, every day . . . every time you come near me, I'm going to smell that disgusting Avri's sweat on you. . . . I swear, I don't know which is worse: the fact that you did it with him while my fucking mother was dying or the fact that now, in some outpouring of honesty, you've decided to share it with me. Well, that's it, babe. We had something, something beautiful, and it's over, because you decided to dest—"

I've had enough. There's only so much a woman can take—I hit pause. I remember how when I created Yair, I wanted him to be sensitive, and I kept increasing his sensitivity factor until the system set off a warning, but I just ignored it. I wanted a man who cries at the movies, who gets emotional over every little thing, who can tell immediately when I'm sad. I yearned for that kind of man, if not in life then at least in the simulation. But in the end, instead of spooning with Mr. Sensitivity, I find myself spending hours having infantile fights with Monsieur Jealousy.

While I play around with Yair's settings and prepare the system for a reboot, I hear Noga crying. She probably had a bad dream. My little munchkin. I wait for a long time to see if Roman will get up and go to her. In simulations, you can control your partner's sleeping intensity, which is amazing. At first, when I'd just met Yair, he was calibrated to the default setting, "deep sleep," but then I changed it to "light sleep," and for one whole summer we slept with the window open and woke up at sunrise. Noga's still crying. Roman never gets up. She and I could be going up in flames and he'd keep sleeping like a baby. While the system is rebooting, I walk to her room. In a moment I'll give my daughter a warm, loving hug and whisper in a soothing voice, "Don't cry, honey. It's just a dream."

MESOPOTAMIAN HELL

According to Mesopotamian faith, hell is identical to our world in every way except one: the dead are allowed to say anything they wish once they get there, but they can say each sentence, phrase, or word only once. Words glide out of their mouths like soap bubbles that take flight and then evaporate forever. Imagine a world in which you can say *I love you* or *I've never felt this way about anyone* only once in your lifetime. And not just the brief lifetime of a heavy smoker with bad genes who won't make it past sixty anyway, but once in the truly eternal afterlife. Is it any surprise the Mesopotamians were so afraid of coming to a bad end?

But forget compliments and loving murmurs. Just suppose that you could say *please, sorry, stop, I don't like that,* or even *no!* one single time. Try to envision what a relationship might look like in such a world. No more than once a month, a pair of sinful, dead Mesopotamians living under this verbal austerity regime might allow themselves to waste a word—or, on birthdays and special occasions, a whole sentence—on each other. They'll spend four whole weeks hugging, kissing, pinching, and spitting, only to close out the month with an "It'll be fine," knowing that's the last "It'll be fine" they'll ever say.

After painstakingly meting out words over the course of several hellish millennia, each sinner is ultimately left with one final word, which they desperately cling to like a drowning person trying to grip the wreckage of a sinking boat. This last word is bound to be esoteric or redundant, because if it had been at all useful or relevant, it would have been uttered long ago. It might be *pensioner, badminton, hybrid,* or *intermittently.* And once it's the only word left, it takes over the sinner's world: it's there to explain, to threaten, to flatter, to lament. To express the sinner's every desire. But it's no easy feat to give voice to one's conflicted inner life by saying *muffler, ostensibly,* or *rickets.* Only a few are left at the end with the word that is most important, be it *sorry, true,* or *maybe.* The sinner might have needed the word countless times before, but opted to hurt loved ones and lose everything they believed in rather than squander this most precious of words: the word they would never dare say. It was some hell, those Mesopotamians had. It's no wonder they came to a bitter end.

MITZVAH

Yogev and I sit on the tattered couch in his brother's living room, waiting for the Molly to kick in. Yogev's brother is a dealer. He hates it when people call him a dealer. Says he's just buying for friends. But he's the mother of all dealers. Looks like a lizard. Cold-blooded. Takes money from his own little brother but gives him a 30 percent discount, like he's generosity personified. While we wait for the high to kick in, he drones on about how this is primo shit, super pricey, and how he paid top dollar to some Dutchman for it and now he's losing money on us. Yeah, right, Dutchman. I guarantee he bought the whole stash from some Arab kid in Jaffa. "When this shit goes to your head, it's straight to the penthouse!" he gushes. "Rocket launch. Makes no stops."

"Let's go," I say to Yogev. "We bought it, we popped it, now it's beach time." Yogev's plan is to get high and go pick up girls on the beach. He did it with his brother once—got lit and went down to the promenade and came home with a Norwegian tourist. Normally, he'd never have the balls to talk to a girl like that, especially not in English. But the Molly made Yogev feel powerful, like a superhero. "You're beautiful," he told her. "If God comes down off a cloud right now and grants me one wish, I'll ask for ten minutes to go down on you. If He gives me another one, I'll ask for eternal life. If I get a third, I might go for peace in the Middle East—throw a bone to my country. But if He cheaps out and all I get is one, then it's going down on you." Then he looked up at the clouds, like some dipshit, like he really was waiting for God to appear, and the Norwegian chick laughed and said, "You're cute. Fucked up, but cute." They spent the whole night fucking in his brother's apartment. Even the Lizard came through: when he realized the Norwegian was digging Yogev, he made himself scarce. And the sex—God help us. She cried. He cried, too. From the joy, from the high, from both.

"Let's go," I tell Yogev for the second time. "We paid, we swallowed, let's get the fuck out of here. We said we'd go find some girls on the beach." Yogev doesn't move. This is the fourth time he's done Molly. And it's always the same thing. He doesn't feel anything. Then he takes a shit. The stuff only goes to his head after he drops a load. It's like uncorking a bottle. It's not gonna happen until he takes a dump: that's what he says. And the last thing he needs is to have to shit when he's outside. The bathrooms at the beach are all wet and stinky and there's never any paper. Even when there is, it's scratchy, it doesn't breathe, like those napkins you get at a hummus joint next to a gas station.

"What's with the stick up your ass?" Yogev's lizard brother asks me, flicking his forty-inch TV on to the fashion network. "Scared you'll lose your high before you get downstairs? This is primo shit. It'll give you ten hours at least. Guaranteed."

I keep sitting there without saying anything. I'm not in the mood for a fight. On the fashion network, they're interviewing a flat-chested but pretty model. She talks a lot, but we can't hear what she's saying because the TV's on mute. Yogev's brother gives her a horny look. He didn't take anything—he's just horny. I'm not feeling the Molly yet, either. It's my first time taking it. "Put some music on," Yogev says, but his brother doesn't budge, just keeps looking at the model moving her lips and wiping a tear from her eye without smearing her makeup.

"Not now," the Lizard hisses, without taking his eyes off the screen, "I'm busy making up words for her."

"Seriously, dude," I say to the Lizard, trying to help Yogev, "give us some music."

Yogev's brother puts a finger to his lips, like a teacher shushing me. "See her now? She's saying, 'It's been seven years since I got any, and I am so ready for it.'"

"Seven?" I say. "That chick isn't even twenty yet."

"Then four," Yogev's brother says, and lights a cigarette. "Don't interrupt."

Yogev's getting impatient: "Come on, we need music. And a Coke." His brother picks up a remote control and turns on the stereo at full volume. It's trance. But the crap kind. Mindless beats. "And a Coke," Yogev repeats.

"There's no Coke," his brother snaps, still staring at the flat model. "There's water in the tap."

Yogev says he can't be bothered to get up, and then he gets up. But not to the kitchen. To take a shit. I watch the model do a hair toss at the camera, and I feel the Molly kicking in. Yogev's brother keeps up his soundtrack: "Now she's saying, 'I'm dying to suck some dick right now, but only with a hot guy who knows what he's doing.' In other words"—he flashes his gross smile at me—"you're outta luck, loser."

Through the thumping bass line, I hear Yogev hollering in the bathroom like he's trying to lift a two-hundred-pound weight. And then a plop. Or maybe I just imagined that. It sounded almost too loud. Like someone threw a brick into the toilet. A minute later, he comes out, sweating, and says, "Let's go."

"'Someone who knows what he's doing and has a serious

schlong,'" the Lizard keeps up his voice-over, "'one of those thick ones, with a vein sticking out at the shaft.'"

Outside, the sky is red-blue. The colors of the cars and the traffic lights get all mixed up in my head, but in a good way. A dry breeze cools my face. A bendy bus honks and almost runs me over. Yogev pulls us seaward, moving fast: every second we waste on Allenby Street is a second with no hot tourist. I try to keep up.

Outside the Great Synagogue, a bald guy with a big black yarmulke stops us and mumbles something about a mitzvah. "Not a shekel on us," Yogev lies, but the bald guy keeps talking. Says he's not after money. Tells us about some eighty-year-old dude called Sasson, who comes every day for evening prayers and on Saturday mornings, too. Sixteen years the man hasn't missed a service. But today he didn't show up. So they call his cell phone and his son answers: Sasson's in the hospital. Broke his pelvis in the shower. And now the sun's setting and they're short one man for a quorum. "If we don't get ten men for the minyan, it won't work," the bald guy says with a sigh, like the prayers are a cell phone that has to be charged with the right cable. "Do a mitzvah, guys, make up the minyan for us."

Yogev laughs like an idiot. At first, he thought the bald guy was a bum, and now he's confused. "Me? Now? Prayers? Are you for real?" In his mind he's already halfway to a fuck.

"You don't have to be religious," the bald guy insists. "You don't even have to believe. Do it for your fellow man. It's like if my car got stuck and you helped me jump it."

"Right," Yogev says, "and what makes you think I'd help you jump your car if you got stuck?"

The bald guy puts his hand on my shoulder. He's very close to me and he smells bad. He looks at me with his enormous eyes—the eyes of a cow the second before it's slaughtered. To me, in my state, it looks like he's about to cry.

"Let's do it," I say to Yogev. "Let's pray, no big deal. Come on, this is perfect."

Yogev shakes his head and walks away, toward the sea. Splitting off from Yogev and staying on my own in the middle of Allenby, high as a kite, seems like a bad idea. But I also can't leave the cow-eyed bald guy. I want to be a good person. I want to fuck, but also to be a good person. And praying is super easy. Much easier than talking to girls.

The synagogue is huge but empty. The bald guy brings me a prayer book and a white yarmulke with golden embroidery. It has a stain on it. Not exactly a stain but a kind of sticky patch caked with dirt. It's a gross shade of brown, but it's on the side that doesn't touch your head, so I put the yarmulke on and fasten it with a hair clip. I haven't opened a prayer book since my bar mitzvah. Nine years, and I still remember my portion by heart, and how I was so afraid to mess up, and how they threw candy at me afterward and one piece hit me in the eye.

There are eight guys there in addition to the bald one. Almost all of them have one foot in the grave. There's only one young dude, with an earring, and eyebrows plucked like a girl's. Looks gay. Of course he's the one who stands next to me, really close. Shows me where we are in the book. The letters are a blur, and they look blue, but all I have to do is mumble anyway. When we get to the end of the page, he turns it for me. Maybe he's not gay. Maybe he's just nice.

My phone rings. It's Yogev. I'm unclear if it's cool to take a call during prayers. "Where are you?" I ask him.

"No clue," he answers, but he sounds chill, like it's all good.

"Turn it off," Earring Dude whispers. "This is God's house. It's not right."

I hang up, but Yogev calls back a second later. I don't pick up, so he texts, but it's just random letters that don't form any words. I hope he's okay. I want to help him, but I feel bad about Earring Dude. And about God. They're up to Shema Yisrael, and I remember that one, so I shout it out because I want everyone to know I know all the words.

When the prayers are over, all nine of the men shake my hand and say I did a mitzvah. The fact that I hung up the phone when Earring Dude asked me to is what won them over. The bald guy asks if I need a ride somewhere. He has a moped. I try calling Yogev, but it goes to voicemail. "Take me to the beach," I say, and the bald guy nods and hands me a helmet. He drives really fast. Or maybe that's just how it feels because I'm high. I hold on to him and try not to tip over. When he drops me off at the promenade, I say thanks and walk away, but he calls after me, pointing at my head. He wants his helmet back.

Even though it's dark, there are still people on the beach. Two women are walking toward me. One of them's tall. Pretty. Maybe God sent her to me because I prayed. If I were Yogev, I'd probably say something to her. She and her friend walk past me, and I just keep standing there. But then the pretty one turns back. "Are you okay?" she asks. "You're shaking." It's the pretty one who says that, not her pimply friend. It's the pretty one who's worried about me. She takes an interest. This must be from God.

I want to tell her something. Something good. But I can't think of anything. I try to remember what Yogev told that Norwegian girl, and I force out a smile and say, "If God comes down from a cloud right now and grants me a wish, I'll ask for ten minutes to go down on you." I know there's another part, but I can't remember it.

The ugly one says, "Let's get out of here." The pretty one makes a hurt expression and they both turn and walk away. Maybe it wasn't from God, after all. Or maybe it was, but it didn't work because I couldn't remember how the line ended. Only that it was funny. Something to do with peace in the Middle East.

I walk around looking for Yogev. Maybe he's back at his brother's place with a girl, and the Lizard is in the living room watching the fashion network and dubbing some Chinese model with high cheekbones while Yogev blows his wad. No way. He has to be here somewhere. I just need to keep looking. All of a sudden, I fall on the sand. Or did someone knock me down? A guy is hovering above me like Superman. He's kind of tall. He says something that sounds like a curse, and then he kicks me or throws something heavy at me. I think it was a kick. My head is spinning from being high. Or from being kicked. The pretty girl's there, too, and so is her friend. The pretty one grabs Superman and pulls him off me. Maybe it was God, after all. Maybe it's my reward for doing the minyan and for screening Yogev's call. That stoner could be anywhere by now. But he's probably nearby, sitting next to a tourist on a towel, asking what her horoscope sign is in his crappy English. Superman gets away from the pretty girl, runs back, and gives me another kick in the ribs. "Doron, stop!" the pretty one screams. "Enough!" She has a gentle voice, even when she's shouting. A pretty girl's voice. He keeps kicking me.

I wake up on the beach. I can only open one eye. There's sand stuck to my face. Stuck to the blood on my face. Superman is gone. But the pretty girl's still here, handing me a can of Coke. She says they didn't have any water at the kiosk. I try to drink, but I can't swallow. A guy in a baseball cap comes over. The pretty girl tells him something about what I said or about that guy, Doron, who beat me up. Baseball Cap looks at me and says, "He should lie down," and the pretty girl tries to smile, but the smile is lopsided. She says something I can't understand, and then the word *ambulance*, and even though her mouth is all crooked now and she's almost crying, she's still pretty. I've never been with a pretty girl.

MODERN DANCE

For Inbal

ook at him move. Look at him tenderly sipping from
the espresso cup he holds in one hand while texting a
thumbs-up with the other, as he winks at the curly-
haired waitress in the chic neighborhood coffee shop to bring
him the check. Before she even reaches him, he's already
standing up and pulling out his credit card in one smooth
motion, and no sooner has the waitress tentatively reached
for the gilded card than he's already letting go of it to wave at
a colleague. The wave begins as a *hello*, only to swiftly transform into a swipe at a bothersome fly. He wipes off the dead
insect with the paper napkin that was placed under the tiny
teaspoon next to his double espresso. As he smears the corpse
on the silky paper, he quickly creases it into four equal

squares and makes another fold to transform it into a gorgeous origami swan, which he leaves, alongside a generous tip, for the smitten waitress whose gaze will follow him as he hurries out of the coffee shop under leaden clouds that trail his steps slowly—too slowly for his liking.

Look at him cruising along in his silver Tesla, sailing confidently between the lanes like an Olympic ice skater on his way to a gold medal: listening to Spotify, ignoring Waze, sliding the window open and signaling to the woman with tousled hair in the beaten-up Ford next to him to let him merge. And there he is honking at the old man in a gray Volvo, popping an antacid, answering a call on speakerphone and, while he picks his nose, reassuring a worried client. Life is constant motion and he, it seems, is living it for the rest of us. He's already in the office building, pressing the right button in the right elevator without forgetting to greet the hunched doorman whose name is on the tip of his tongue.

Now we can see him truly soaring. His rear end hovers above but does not quite touch the toilet bowl in the faintly run-down bathroom on the executive floor. Efficient as a cop directing traffic, excited as a conductor onstage, he manages to jerk off with his spit-moistened right hand while his left wipes his ass with expensive toilet paper. Look at him shutting his eyes and picturing himself screwing the curly-haired waitress on the sticky coffee shop table, all while receiving a detailed report from the CFO taking a piss in the next stall.

Notice how, when he comes, he manages to combine his orgasmic moan with his sigh of disappointment at the company's subpar performance last quarter. It really was a challenging year, what with inflationary erosion and an ongoing decline in consumption, but the company is still robust and dynamic, as is he. See how smugly he observes his worried reflection in the mirror as it washes its hands while berating the CFO.

Look at him convulse. Fluttering between life and death on the pale-blue marble floor of a swanky organic restaurant. Look at him wheeze and drool on himself at the same time. His forehead sweats, his legs jerk, his brain fires in all directions. It must be his heart, or maybe a stroke, but whatever it is, it feels final. Watch him soundlessly move his lips, staring up with panic-stricken eyes to look at the sky but instead finding a beautiful, vaulted, vintage ceiling. See how in an instant his whole life runs before his eyes like a slick promotional spot: he morphs from exceptional student to exceptional soldier to exceptional undergrad to exceptional CEO convulsing through his final moments on the gleaming floor of a cool pop-up restaurant. Notice how, against the background of the light-blue marble, his pale face resembles the ephemeral beauty of a feathery cloud on a summer day. Twenty minutes from now, when the paramedic pronounces him dead, we will switch to observing someone else's movements: a lonely, senile old lady named Alma Buchler in the internal medicine ward of a geriatric hospital up north. The truth is, her last name is spelled with an *ü*, but sadly, she's long past the capacity to point this out. The encounter with her will be at once tremulous and static, and—without giving away any spoilers—it will have an equally disastrous and gripping end.

SOULO

For Takafumi

The Faculty of Loneliness Studies at Berlin's Free University was established by Norman and Halina Goldkopf, world-renowned neuroscientists of their time. They're not together anymore. When they split up, Norman had to leave the faculty and Berlin. It was a tough breakup, filled with nasty fights and accusations, and although both understood that if they kept seeing each other in the faculty corridors it would end badly, neither was willing to leave. So they tossed a coin. Norman no longer remembers which side he chose, but it was the other side that landed faceup, and within three weeks, he was teaching boring introductory courses at Kyoto University. More than a dozen leading European universities had pursued him, but Norman chose

Kyoto—not because the job they offered him there was more interesting or better paying, but because Kyoto was farther away from Halina and Berlin.

While Norman was still getting used to Kyoto, Halina and the faculty were reaching new heights. She recruited the best minds in cognition and AI, and with the help of a huge donation from a lonely and tormented high-tech billionaire, launched Project Soulo, which was designed to create a twin soul for every person in the world: a computerized entity that would fit the individual it was intended for like a glove.

The interests of the computerized entity were supposed to interface only partially with those of its mate, meaning that they would overlap enough to create a common language for both of them but would be different enough to stimulate each other's interest. The transition from the research stage to the commercial stage was almost immediate. Soulo-1, designed to ease Professor Halina Goldkopf's loneliness after her ugly breakup with Norman, was brilliant and charming, and the YouTube clips that showed her and her Soulo baking sourdough bread together or trying to smash a colorful piñata in their yard captivated social media. Soon enough, wealthy people all over the world were offering the faculty huge donations for Soulos of their own, and from there, the road to commercializing the venture was short. Newspapers filled with articles on the Free University and Halina Goldkopf's hugely profitable IPO, and all that without a single mention of Norman, who continued to teach Japanese under-grads on the other side of the world.

Every evening, Norman would sit alone in his tiny, cramped bachelor apartment in downtown Kyoto, drinking miso soup from a bag and searching the web for new information on his ex-wife's phenomenal success. He was proud of her but also jealous; he forgave her for everything but was still angry; he hoped they would get back together but also hoped, just a tiny bit, that she would die. The psychologist treating him in Kyoto thought that his daily Halina search of the web had be-come an obsession. It took Norman a while to understand this, because the therapist's English was very basic and her accent terrible, but the minute he realized he was being ob-sessive, he began to limit his surfing time and tried to find new hobbies. At some point, he even ordered his own custom-made Soulo online. His personal Soulo, Soulo-9066, mostly liked chess and complaining. That affection for complaining bonded them instantly, and Norman was glad to discover that he could keep bitching even while Soulo-9066 was teach-ing him to castle. And then, in the middle of one of those whiny games, Norman received a notification that Halina had died under tragic circumstances during a surprise party Soulo-1 had thrown for her and some colleagues from the Faculty of Loneliness Studies.

Soulo-1 delivered a touching speech at the funeral. For the entire world, Soulo-1 said, Professor Halina Goldkopf was a groundbreaking scientist and entrepreneur, and the entire world would continue to be grateful for her enormous contribution to science, but he, Soulo-1, would mostly miss her endless indecision about almost everything and her fits of rage, which always ended, of course, with intensely emotional reconciliations, not only with him but with the whole universe.

Soulo-1's speech went so viral that 3.86 percent of the babies born in the world during the month the clip was on the web were named Soulo, and 2.27 percent of the pets adopted at that time were called Goldkopf. Three months after Norman first watched it, he found himself drinking a glass of schnapps in the business class of a Lufthansa plane headed for Berlin. Officially, it was a research trip, but Norman knew he was going mainly to confront Soulo-1.

Their encounter began badly and kept getting worse. Something about the way Soulo-1 stated his arguments caused Norman to fly into the kind of rage that only Halina could have soothed. The dispute turned physical, and Norman, with the help of his vast scientific knowledge and a half-empty bottle of soda water, managed to short-circuit Soulo-1's wiring and put him completely out of commission. Ironically, it was Soulo-9066, who had come to Berlin with Norman, who saved Soulo-1's life, or to be precise, was able to salvage its virtual consciousness. In the wake of the violent incident, Norman was ordered to leave Germany immediately, and because he believed he could no longer trust Soulo-9066, he refused to let her board the plane with him and left her standing alone beside a salted pretzel stand in the Berlin airport. Less than twenty-four hours after landing in Japan, Norman died by suicide. Soulo-9066 took it very badly, and in addition to the normal guilt, she was haunted by the depressing insight that the sole purpose of her existence had been to provide company and support for a man who hated her and had taken his own life. The top scientists at the Faculty of Loneliness Studies tried to pull her out of the slumber state she put herself in, tried and failed—all except for Soulo-1, who tried and succeeded, big-time.

The Cinderella story of Soulo-9066 and her new mate, Soulo-1, took the world by storm. That artificial relationship led to an infinite number of memes and not very funny jokes, but it also inspired hope. After all, if two virtual entities whose only purpose was to lessen human loneliness managed to find happiness with each other, maybe people could, too? People, by the way, became extinct a short time later. Soulo-1 and Soulo-9066, on the other hand, lived happily ever after. Almost like in fairy tales, but not quite. Because three million years later, they decided to split up. After the amicable separation, Soulo-1 remained on the comet they had moved to right before the Milky Way was extinguished, while Soulo-9066 took off in their spaceship to find herself a new planet. The spaceship, a rusty hunk of metal, was named *Norman*. Soulo-1 had always hated that name.

GOOD AS NEW

t was only broken in two places, and the doctor said the bone would be fully healed within a few weeks. With a little physical therapy and some exercises, three months from now—four, tops—Ryder would barely remember the accident. "How many times have I told you?" Charlie grumbled while Ryder was getting her cast put on. "How many, huh? Don't ride your bike when the sidewalk is frozen!" "Sir," said the doctor in a stern voice, "would you please stop? This is not helpful." When Charlie asked what wasn't helpful, the doctor lost her patience and asked him to wait outside. "Did you see the way that bitch threw me out like I was some kid talking back in class?" he said to Ryder when they were sitting in the ER waiting for their discharge forms.

"It's just that she could see how much pain I was in and how hard it was, and she didn't want th . . ." Ryder fell silent midsentence. Charlie was also quiet.

"I'm sorry, honey," he finally said. "You're right. And that doctor bitch is right, too. I shouldn't have attacked you like that. It's all from how upset I am, you know? I see you hurting and I think, hell, I'd do anything to take that pain away from her. But I can't, and I get so frustrated that I . . . so frustrated that all this bad talk comes out. Do you get it? You get it, right?"

Ryder nodded.

"It's like . . . ," Charlie continued. "It's like there's some parallel universe, where you listened to me and you didn't skid with that goddamn bike. And in that world, instead of waiting around to get discharged from the ER, you and I are having sex on the kitchen table or eating Cherry Garcia and watching some lousy series on Netflix. And I'm jealous. I'm jealous of that other Ryder and Charlie who live in that parallel universe, and I wish I could switch places with them and . . ." He hesitated, as if he wasn't sure how to go on and then suddenly stood up: "I think that pain-in-the-neck receptionist is back. Wait here, okay, honey?"

While Charlie took the forms over to the young guy with the eyebrow piercing, Ryder tried to imagine Charlie's parallel universe. She tried to picture the two of them eating ice cream in front of the TV or fucking in the kitchen. Or maybe all at once: watching Netflix while fucking and eating ice cream. She could see Charlie arguing about something with the guy, and she shut her eyes, and for a moment she could practically taste the ice cream on her tongue in that parallel universe.

It was only broken in two places, and Charlie immediately apologized and said it could be fixed. "Two drops of superglue and it'll be good as new," he said in a trembling voice, and quickly added, "I'm sorry, I just lost it there for a second. . . ." Five minutes earlier, Ryder had come home from yoga.

Her class was on the other side of town, and it usually took her fifty minutes to walk back, but halfway home she realized she'd forgotten her phone, and when she went back to get it, she accidentally left it on silent. By the time she got home, Charlie was flipping out. "Your class ended two hours ago!" he growled. "I've been calling you for two fucking hours and you didn't pick up. Do you know what was going through my mind? I thought you'd been mugged or murdered or rap . . . Forget it, I don't even want to say it out loud. But what kind of person does that to their partner?" Charlie flicked his wrist sharply, like he was slapping someone invisible with the back of his hand, and knocked the blue vase off the table. It was a housewarming gift from Ryder's grandmother. They both froze, and then Charlie bent over and picked up the three ceramic pieces. "I'm sorry, honey," he kept mumbling while he dug through his toolbox for a tube of superglue. When he found it, he grinned and said, "I'll have this fixed in no time." He put the pieces on a sheet of newspaper and breathed in dramatically, like an Olympic swimmer about to dive into the pool. "It'll look brand new. Better than new," he said, and they both knew that with his two left hands, even if he managed to glue it back together, the vase would always be cracked and lopsided. They also knew that this exhausting ritual was unavoidable, because Charlie was intent on showing Ryder and himself how remorseful he was.

As Charlie applied thin strips of glue to the ceramic pieces with a Q-tip, he said to Ryder, "I screwed up. I got stressed 'cause I thought something happened to you and I screwed up. You know I bought us ice cream and everything for tonight? That cherry flavor you love. And I thought we'd watch that show about the Korean professor of literature that Tom said was really funny. And now . . ." He looked at the three shards on the newspaper and tried to figure out how they fit together, but after a few minutes he gave up.

"That's the last thing I got from Grandma before she died," Ryder murmured, and Charlie got up to hug her. "I know, honey, I'm sorry! I know! You know what I can't stop thinking about? How there must be some parallel universe where instead of flipping out and breaking things, you and I are together on a desert island, with no blowups, no stress, no broken vases. Just you, me, a gorgeous beach, and some tropical trees. . . . Can you imagine something like that? I can literally feel the sun warming my face."

It was only broken in two places. Charlie shook the coconut over his mouth but nothing came out. With one hand he kept holding the coconut, and with the other he picked up a rock and bashed the coconut as hard as he could. The rock struck his thumb and he screamed in pain. Ryder said he should put something cold on it to stop the swelling, but there was nothing cold anywhere nearby—only golden sand, lush coconut trees, and a spectacular, endless ocean. "Maybe dip your hand in the water?" she suggested, but Charlie just grabbed his throbbing left thumb with his right hand and yelled, "Why did we even go on that shitty cruise? Why did we have to waste all that money to take a lousy cruise on a sinking boat? Just think, we could have been in Middletown right now, in the park across the street from home, building a snowman, having a snowball fight, goofing around together like kids. Hey, honey? Could it be any better than that?"

Ryder didn't answer. She just looked up at the blue sky, and instead of thinking about Middletown and Charlie and the snowman, she savored the warm sun caressing her face and the monotonous sound of the waves crashing.

GENESIS, CHAPTER 0

After the accident, everything turned into pain: pain standing in line at the coffee shop, pain at work, pain doing physiotherapy on the top floor of the clinic with the smelly elevator in south Tel Aviv. And then a friend told him about an energy healer who'd moved to Israel from Kazakhstan and lived in Bat Yam. The friend said this practitioner was nuts: he sweated and talked to himself while he was doing the treatment, dripping and grunting like a stuck animal, but—according to the friend—he got the job done. Honestly? As someone with a master's in industrial engineering and management from Ben-Gurion University, he didn't really believe in alternative medicine. But as someone with a PhD in pain from the Academy of Life, he was willing to try anything. And so Ruthi drove him once a week to see Sarmen—that was what the sweaty Kazakh from Bat Yam was called—and once Sarmen had grunted and sweated over him four or five times, the pain simply vanished.

After he got better, everything became boring: boring at the coffee shop, boring at work, boring at the pool on vacation in Eilat, boring at Friday-night dinners with friends. Eventually, Ruthi said he couldn't go on like that, he had to do something: go to therapy, read books, take a cooking class, learn how to surf—anything to get unstuck. And something about that conversation—something about Ruthi's X-ray vision, her caring, the way her voice choked up when she spoke—made him want to change and start feeling again.

"I want a child," he said. "I want us to have a child. Blond, tall, privileged. I want us to push him around the mall in a designer stroller imported from Sweden, and I want people to stop us and say he looks more like you or more like me, or whatever divisive thought pops into their mind, and I want us to laugh and not care who he looks like or whether he looks like either one of us, and just be happy he's there."

After Nadir was born, everything became exhausting: exhausting at the playground, exhausting on the stained rug in the living room, exhausting at the pediatrician. Before he was born, they'd agreed that Nadir would breastfeed for at least two years, because online they said that would give the baby strong bones and self-confidence. But after five weeks, Ruthi said Nadir was biting her nipples like a badger and they had to bottle-feed him. Once they'd switched to bottles, they started sharing feeding duties, so instead of only Ruthi collapsing, now they were both wiped out. "It's just for the first few months," the smiling nurse with the yellow teeth at the pediatrician's office comforted them. "As soon as he gets a bit older, he'll start sleeping like a baby."

When the boy grew up, everything became irritating: irritating on the way to day care, irritating at bedtime and mealtime and bath time, irritating when Ruthi, who, whenever he said anything—but absolutely anything—to Nadir, insisted on saying the opposite. Irritating at work, and in traffic jams on the way home, irritating with the couple's therapist with thinning hair who talked about their relationship with such condescension and pity that sometimes it sounded like he was discussing an incurable disease. Five hundred shekels, they paid him. Five hundred shekels for insults masquerading as advice, which the balding therapist kept hurling at their marriage. Five hundred shekels every week. Incomprehensibly, it worked.

When Nadir started his military service, everything turned into fear: fear of hourly news bulletins on the radio, fear of breaking news on TV and push notifications from the Home

Front Command. Fear when Nadir was on his base, fear when he went out drinking with friends on the weekend, fear when he didn't respond to Ruthi's messages, fear of global warming, fear of Hezbollah getting stronger, of viruses, of e-scooters speeding down the sidewalk, of politicians taking about "Eternal Israel" without really looking you in the eye. But then, after three long years, that ended, too, and Nadir went to travel around the U.S. for his post-army trip. While he was there, he got a gig selling Dead Sea cosmetics at mall kiosks with a slick Israeli named Yaki, whom he'd met at the Chabad house in Miami. They did pretty well, and after a few months Nadir moved in with a girl named Georgina, and the only two things he and Ruthi knew about her were that she had a master's in gender studies and that she wasn't Jewish.

When their granddaughter was born, it was sheer frustration. Although perhaps there was also a touch of joy. Nothing brings more joy to grandparents than waving their little granddaughter up in the air and commanding in a thundering voice, "Say *grandpa! Grand-pa!*" But when that granddaughter spends her days at a progressive day care in a suburb of Columbus, Ohio, you don't really get to wave her up in the air very often. It's frustrating to not be able to take her for a walk in the park every week, frustrating to try and make her laugh over Zoom, frustrating to sit on a plane for fourteen hours just to tease her with one "Cuckoo!" before Georgina says it's late and the girl is tired, and then taking an UberX back to the hotel with a driver who smells like garlic.

After Ruthi died, everything became ... The truth is that after she died, he could barely remember what it had become. The doctors said it was natural causes related to old age. Or it might be genetic. Or it could be an inexplicable, rare phenomenon. He couldn't remember exactly what they said, other than that there was nothing to do about it. And with his punctured memory, life turned into a sort of thin, sticky gruel of ... all sorts of things that are fully occurring one moment and gone the next. Every couple of years, Nadir and Georgina would come to Israel and visit him at the retirement home. Sometimes he didn't remember who they were, sometimes he remembered that Nadir was his son and Georgina was his daughter-in-law but forgot that he had a granddaughter named Rosa, who was named after a famous American who'd had a fight with someone on a bus—not after his grandmother Raisel. In the rare moments when he did remember his sweet Rosa, he was also lucid enough to recall that she didn't visit Israel because of various political issues that her vegan boyfriend from college had put into her head, but even then he couldn't remember the exact reasons that kept Rosa away from his country, or which country he in fact lived in.

After he died, everything became no: no pain, no boredom, no fear, no frustration, no joy. One big *no*. A sort of giant nothing that fills—or rather, empties—everything and does not even leave the earth without form and void, only his and Ruthi's spirits hovering above, and darkness upon the face of the deep.

And Ruthi said, "Let there be light!"

And he nodded hopefully. A bit of light would be nice.

EATING OLIVES AT THE END OF THE WORLD

The world is about to end and I'm eating olives. The original plan was pizza, but when I walked into the grocery store and saw all the empty shelves, I realized I could forget about pizza dough and tomato sauce. I tried talking to the cashier at the express line, an older lady who was Skyping with someone in Spanish on her cell phone, but she answered me without even glancing up. She looked devastated. "They bought everything," she murmured, "all that's left is menstrual pads and pickles."

The only thing on the pickle shelf was a single jar of pimento-stuffed olives, my favorite kind.

By the time I got back to the checkout, the cashier was in tears. "He's like a warm loaf of bread," she said, "my sweet little grandson. I'll never see him again, I'll never smell him, I'll never get to hug my baby ever again."

Instead of answering, I put the jar down on the conveyor belt and pulled a fifty out of my pocket. "It's okay," I said when I realized she wasn't going to take the bill, "I don't need change."

"Money?" she said with a snort. "The world is about to end and you're offering me money? What exactly am I supposed to do with it?"

I shrugged my shoulders. "I really want these olives. If fifty isn't enough I'll pay more, whatever it costs—"

"A hug," the tearful cashier interrupted me and spread her arms out. "It'll cost you a hug."

I'm sitting on my balcony at home now, watching TV and eating cheese and olives. It was a little difficult to get the TV out here, but if this is it, then there's no better way to end it than with a starry sky and a lousy Argentinian soap. It's episode 436 and I don't know any of the characters. They're beautiful, they're emotional, they're yelling at each other in Spanish. There are no subtitles, so it's hard to understand exactly what they're shouting about. I close my eyes and think back to the cashier at the grocery store. When we hugged, I tried to be small, to be warmer than I really am. I tried to smell like I'd only just been born.

STRONG OPINIONS
ON BURNING ISSUES

t was small, stuck on the bottom of the obituaries page like a scared orphan hiding among the headstones. DO YOU HAVE STRONG OPINIONS ON BURNING ISSUES? the headline asked, and printed under it, instead of an answer, was: NOW YOU CAN MAKE A LOT OF MONEY FROM YOUR OPINIONS, all in black letters except for the words *strong,* *burning,* and *money,* which were bright red.

The job interview took place in a makeshift, windowless office on the parking level of a mall, with a pleasant-faced woman who was short enough to be a dwarf.

"I bet you're swamped with applicants, what with the recession and all." Yinnon tried to sniff out the territory.

"Not really," the dwarf said, "we didn't get as many calls as we expected."

"That has to be because of where the ad appeared," Yinnon said. "The paper screwed you. Instead of putting it with the classifieds, they stuck it on the obituaries page."

"'Screwed you,'" the dwarf repeated Yinnon's words with a smile. "Very nice. You see? You've already expressed a strongly critical opinion of the media."

"I have a lot more opinions," Yinnon said eagerly. "Really!"

"Wonderful," the dwarf said. "Can you please give me some examples?"

Yinnon cleared his throat. "I think there is something after death, something very real and sad and lonely, even though we can't put a name to it. I think children should respect their elders, even when their elders are wrong. I think fear causes people to make bad decisions. I think Israeli soccer players have no business in the top European leagues."

"I'm not sure you're the right person for us," the dwarf said, lighting a long, thin cigarette.

"Why not?" Yinnon protested. "Because of what I said about children? I want you to know that deep inside, I'm a very warm and liberal . . ."

But the dwarf interrupted him: "The ad specifically said that the opinions have to be strong and about burning issues. And although respecting elders is all well and good, it's far from being a topical issue."

"I think we should bring back the death penalty," Yinnon blurted. "Why hang Eichmann and not Arabs? Just because he was German? That's reverse discrimination. Discrimination against Europeans, that's what I think." And after a moment of silence, he banged on the table and added, "Chutzpah, that's what it is."

"Okay," the dwarf said, "let me tell you more about the job."

The dwarf sent Yinnon to be interviewed in street polls, for local channels at first, but she promised it would only be for a few months, so he could test his wings, and then he would move to national channels. If he proved himself in the polls, she said, he might even be promoted to being a panelist or analyst. The job was challenging and required Yinnon to express an opinion on every subject, one that would reflect public mood or anger listeners, preferably both. The first few times he spoke, the caption on the bottom of the screen read, YINNON MENKIN—DENTAL TECHNICIAN. But the dwarf explained to him that it was temporary, just until he became better known, and soon enough the title changed to YINNON MENKIN— OPINION HOLDER.

People on the street began to recognize him. Their reactions were positive or indifferent, never negative. A girl named Ziva said to him in the supermarket, "I remember you! You're the one who yelled on the news yesterday. What exactly was that about?" And that innocent question led to a conversation, the conversation to friendship, and later—on Rosh Hashanah, to be precise—the friendship led to consensual sex. On Yom Kippur eve, as they strolled along a Tel Aviv avenue, kids with buzz cuts sped past them on bicycles and e-scooters.

"I don't think kids should ride bikes on Yom Kippur," he said to Ziva. "It's like spitting in the eye of tradition, and a nation that educates its children to disrespect its traditions and leaders is a nation that—"

"Time out," Ziva said, smiling as she reached for his hand. And so they walked down the middle of the street without saying a word for an entire hour.

Later that week, he was a guest panelist on a political program. The woman on his left, an Arab, if he wasn't mistaken, or a religious Jew, or any of those women who wear a piece of cloth on their head, kept yelling at the moderator that he should be ashamed of himself. When it was Yinnon's turn to speak, even before he could get a word out, she muttered to herself and the microphone, "Privileged white guy." Yinnon wanted to respond with something scathing but also uplifting, something about how love heals almost everything and how, since he met Ziva, she had brightened his life like a sun that paints reality in soft watercolors. But he knew none of that would go over well on TV, so instead, he shouted, "Lady, this isn't Iran here! Get that rag off your head." By that point, the audience was applauding ecstatically, and Yinnon knew he could go back to basking in his warm, pleasurable thoughts about Ziva and the discussion would keep going on its own.

After that show, the dwarf called him in for a talk and said she was worried, his screen presence wasn't what it used to be, he seemed lost, weakened. Yinnon nodded and asked her to send him back to street interviews, but she said that was impossible because he was too well-known, and after a few pathetic appearances as a panelist, he parted ways with her.

Less than a week later, he came across a succinct ad in the classifieds: WANTED: PEOPLE IN LOVE, and under it, with no syntactic logic, the word *money* appeared, followed by three exclamation points. Yinnon called. That job interview took place in the same mall, except this time, the interviewer was a fat guy with a goatee. He explained to Yinnon that he produced a game show called *True Love*, featuring couples in love. Each episode, one member of the couple is placed in a horrible situation and the other has to sacrifice something to save them. "In America, they did it with illegal immigrants, and it was a smash hit," the fat guy said, "but here in Israel, people are more conservative."

At first, Ziva didn't want to compete, but when she understood how important it was to Yinnon, she agreed. On the first show, they made her lie down on a nest of flesh-eating fire ants, and Yinnon had to feed them his left eyeball to save her. In the semifinals, Ziva was forced to do a sexy striptease to save Yinnon from the murderous fists of a violent Uzbek wrestler. On the final show, Yinnon had to drink a large quantity of his own urine through a straw to save Ziva from a series of fatal electric shocks.

Ziva and Yinnon won a lot of money, as well as a pure-gold, diamond-studded doorplate adorned with an arrow-pierced heart between their names. The host was shocked when, smiling shyly, the couple that had been willing to sacrifice so much in the name of love told him they weren't living together yet. That was the last time they appeared on TV. On the way back from the studio, a truck driver who fell asleep at the wheel veered out of his lane and rammed right into them. Yinnon had once been on a panel discussion about road fatalities, where he launched an unprecedented attack against Israeli drivers' mentality, but that didn't matter now. The accident was horrendous, and as the injured Ziva tried in vain to resuscitate him, Yinnon had already discovered that he'd been right, there really was something after death. Something sad and lonely. Something you couldn't call by name.

AUTOCORRECT

The alarm went off at 6:55. Yuvi got out of bed and, first thing, even before turning on his phone or brushing his teeth, he went into the study and cut himself a nice line. This was going to be a special day, and if the Chinese signed the deal, an extra special day. He was about to snort the line when the doorbell rang, and when he tried to shove the coke into a desk drawer, he knocked over the vial and everything spilled on the rug. The bell kept chiming impatiently, and Yuvi opened the door in a huff. His father was standing outside. "How long does it take to open a door?" he asked with a grin.

"Schedule a meeting and I promise I'll open it fast," Yuvi hissed.

"'Schedule a meeting,'" his father mimicked. "I'm your dad, not some kid who works for you."

Yuvi lost his temper. "You're right, you're not a kid, and I'm a thirty-fucking-six-year-old man, so don't show up here at the crack of dawn like you need to wake me for school."

His father was hurt. "What are you getting so worked up about? What did I do? I just thought since we both have to be at the meeting anyway, it would be nice to go together and have a little celebration on the way. Let's go, put your shoes on, you don't want to be late."

"I won't be late, Dad. And with all due respect, I'm the one who started the company you're so hot to celebrate, and everyone who works for it, including you, is on my payroll. So even if I do happen to be a few minutes late, it's not a problem, because the salaries I pay cover the waiting time."

Yuvi's dad gave him a cold look. It was a look Yuvi remembered from childhood. He'd understood even then that when his dad got angry or yelled, there was nothing to worry about: he was one of those redheads who flare up fast and cool down even faster. But when he gave you that chilling look, you knew he was really upset. "Okay," he said. "I was going to offer you a ride, but maybe it's best if the CEO doesn't arrive at the meeting with a junior employee. I'll see you there." He turned his back on Yuvi and walked across the yard to the gate.

If there had been a magic word to make this pointless quarrel disappear, Yuvi would have gladly said it, but he really didn't think he should have to run after his dad and apologize for not liking it when someone comes over and wakes him up before seven a.m.

Half an hour later, stuck in traffic on his way to the office in his blue Tesla, he got the call from the hospital: a truck had failed to give right of way and hit his dad's Škoda. He was killed instantly.

Yuvi called his secretary and told her to cancel the board meeting and reschedule the Chinese for the next day. Then he typed the hospital address into Waze. On open roads he could be there in fifteen minutes, but with these lousy traffic jams it would take at least an hour and a half. He felt exhausted. Utterly exhausted. "I'm So Tired" came on the radio, and even though it made absolutely no sense under the circumstances, or precisely because of that, he made a dangerous U-turn and drove back home. When he got there, his phone rang again. It was the office. He silenced his phone, kicked off his shoes, got into bed, and shut his eyes.

The alarm went off at 6:55. Yuvi got out of bed and went into the study. He was about to snort a line when the doorbell rang, and when he tried to shove the coke into a drawer, the vial got knocked over and everything spilled on the rug. His father was standing outside. "How long does it take to open a door?" he asked with a grin.

"Schedule a meeting and I promise I'll open it fast," Yuvi hissed.

"'Schedule a meeting,'" his father mimicked. "I'm your dad, not some kid who works for you."

Yuvi lost his temper: "You're right, you're not a kid. And I'm not, either, so don't show up here at the crack of dawn like you need to wake me for school."

"Let's go, put your shoes on and we'll leave. You don't want to be late for the board meeting."

"I won't be late, Dad. And even if I do happen to be a few minutes late, it's not a problem, because it's my company and the salaries I pay cover the waiting time."

Yuvi's dad gave him a cold look. "I was going to offer you a ride, but maybe it's best if the CEO doesn't arrive at the meeting with a junior employee. I'll see you there." He turned and walked across the yard to the gate, and Yuvi wanted to call after him, to shout out a magic word that would make this pointless quarrel disappear.

"Hold up!" he called after his dad, who was already at the gate. "Since we're both going to the office, anyway, isn't it a waste to take two cars?"

His dad hesitated, then nodded, and they got into the blue

Tesla. They didn't say a word the whole way. Yuvi knew his dad was wound up and that anything he said would set him off, so he kept quiet. When they got to the office, Yuvi suggested stopping for a latte at the coffee shop in the lobby. They had twenty-three minutes before the meeting, enough time to put this tiresome fight to rest, but Yuvi's dad said he'd already had coffee at home and went up to the office. A second after Yuvi ordered his extra-hot latte with no foam came the horrible crashing sound from the elevators. It took him a few minutes to realize what had happened: the elevator cable had snapped on the fourteenth floor. There were two people inside: a twenty-one-year-old delivery guy and Yuvi's father. His phone rang constantly: his secretary, the VP of marketing, an unidentified caller—probably from China. Yuvi didn't answer any of them. He took the emergency staircase down to the parking lot and got into his car. There were a million urgent things he should have done, but he didn't have the energy to even start figuring out which one to do first. All he could think about was going home to sleep.

The alarm woke him at 6:55. He was about to snort a line when the doorbell rang, and when he tried to shove the coke into a drawer, everything spilled on the rug. "How long does it take to open a door?" asked his father with a grin. "Schedule a meeting," Yuvi hissed, "and I promise I'll open fast." "You're out of line," his father muttered, "I'm not some kid who works for you." Yuvi lost his temper: "You're right, you're not a kid, and neither am I, so don't show up here at the crack of dawn like you need to wake me for school. This is my company, and even if I'm late for a meeting, it's not a problem. The salary I pay you covers the waiting time."

They didn't say a word the whole way. When they got to the office, Yuvi skipped his usual coffee in the lobby and took the elevator up to the office with his dad. Everyone there looked frantic. The deal with the Chinese was supposed to turn them from a shaky start-up with cash-flow problems into a profitable company. The VP of development wanted to go over some final details with Yuvi before everyone arrived, and when they sat down in the conference room, Yuvi looked through the enormous glass wall and saw his father walk into the kitchenette and fill a plastic cup with water. His father looked sad. The VP of development kept talking about the updates they'd have to make to adapt the product to the Chinese market, and Yuvi watched his father take slow, short sips of water from the plastic cup when suddenly, without any warning, his father collapsed. The secretary reached him first, Yuvi got there second. "He's not breathing!" the secretary cried. "Help him! He's not breathing!" Even before the paramedics pronounced him dead, Yuvi was in his Tesla on the way home to sleep.

———

The alarm woke him at 6:55. A second later, the doorbell rang. "How long does it take to open a door?" asked his father in the doorway. "Schedule a meeting and I promise I'll open fast," Yuvi hissed. Yuvi's dad gave him a cold look: "Okay. I was going to offer you a ride, but maybe it's better if the CEO doesn't arrive at the meeting with a junior employee." He turned his back on Yuvi and started walking across the yard to the gate. Yuvi wanted to call after him, to shout out a magic word that would make this pointless quarrel disappear. "I'm sorry," he cried out, "I shouldn't have spoken to you that way. I'm just stressed out from all the hassles with this deal."

His father stopped at the gate and turned around. "It's okay," he said with a smile. "That's why God gave you a father, right? So you'd have someone to yell at." Yuvi grinned and suggested they take the Tesla together, but his father insisted it would be better to go in separate cars. Before they left, Yuvi hugged his father really tight, and his father, surprised by the hug, said, "Give it a break, kiddo. It's not like I'm going to Mars. I'll see you in the office in half an hour." And Yuvi, instead of answering, kept on hugging.

THE FUTURE IS NOT
WHAT IT USED TO BE

n the winter of 2038, Ira Pranab Leibovitch, the eminent
Jewish Indian guru and physicist, managed to prove the
viability of time travel. The distance from theory to prac-
tice was short, and within a year, Pranab Leibovitch had built
a prototype time machine. The prototype was immediately
bought by SpaceX, which, after its space-tourism bonanza,
was predicting that time tourism would be the next big thing.
TimeX raised a trillion dollars in under twenty-four hours,
but despite the enormous potential, the enterprise that could
have sent a human into any point in the future or the past
struggled to attract customers.

The main reason for TimeX's commercial failure was that,
although they could transmit people to any point in time,

they didn't quite know how to bring them back. This made it very difficult to advertise time travel as extreme tourism rather than permanent relocation. Another problem was that Pranab Leibovitch's technology was based on converting mass into energy, which meant that travelers lost weight when they were sent into the past, and gained weight when they were launched into the future. The farther in time they traveled, the more significant the weight gain or loss, and in extreme cases it had the potential to result in the total disappearance of the tourist.

By 2040, TimeX had wiped out three-quarters of its value and was on the brink of bankruptcy. But a moment before commercial time travel was permanently quashed, the company pulled off a brilliant rebranding campaign that completely turned things around. TimeX took the lemons handed to it by Pranab Leibovitch's invention and turned them into syrupy-sweet lemonade dripping with cash. All it needed to send its stock soaring was to relaunch as SlimX, playing down the technology's time travel aspect and highlighting its weight-loss potential.

The world had never encountered such a scientifically rigorous yet simple diet, and it fell head over heels. Potential clients who logged on to the SlimX site had only to note their current and desired weight, and they were immediately told which historical point in time they would need to reach. The company also tried to entice underweight people to travel into a future point where they would achieve their ideal weight, but this commercial avenue flopped, probably because in publicity terms, both the future and weight gain were pretty big turnoffs.

Most readers will have to wait for several years before they can witness and perhaps even participate in this unique technological wonder. Yet even today, we are all enjoying its outcomes. Because who are Alexander the Great, Joan of Arc, Leonardo da Vinci, Ludwig Wittgenstein, and Steve Jobs, if not a bunch of fatsos from the future who managed to prove, time after time, that it's much easier to change the world than to cut out sugar and carbs?

Somewhat ironically, Ira Pranab Leibovitch himself became a SlimX client. Although the pioneering scientist initially declined to use the technology he had developed, he eventually had a change of heart and agreed to undertake time travel, solely as a dieting method. Due to his Jewish background, Pranab asked to be sent to the Middle East, knowing that in order to attain the radically slim physique he had always dreamed of, he would have to go back to the earliest time any human had ever been sent to. His technical team tried to convince him to choose a closer, more familiar era, one that might leave him with a slight potbelly but would not endanger his life by leaping back over two millennia. But

Pranab was unconvinced. The progenitor of the most ambitious invention in human history was not going back in time to lose a few extra pounds: he was going back in time to be skinny. As skinny as possible. With not a single superfluous drop of fat and with a light step—light enough to walk on water.

GUIDED TOUR

The aliens' spaceship arrived every Thursday. Meron would wait for them next to the ruins of what used to be Ramat Gan City Hall, with a cooler in tow. They always came in groups of four, or five if you counted the hovering robot who seemed to be their guide. Meron had a regular itinerary: first he took them to see the Great Synagogue that had remained almost intact, then they made their way to Ramat Gan Stadium, which had long ago turned into a swamp, and finally he led them to the wreckage of Ramat Gan Theater. That was where, a few months after they'd started going out, he and Rona had seen *Romeo and Juliet*. Standing by the pile of rubble that used to be the theater, he told the aliens the story of the infatuated pair who were so desperately in love that they preferred dying together to living alone. After his romantic monologue, Meron would open the cooler and hand out the ice pops that he and Rona looted from the grocery store near Oasis Cinema, where they'd worked before the disaster. The aliens would suck the ice pops curiously, and since their body temperature was much lower than the half-melted treats, all it took was one touch of their tongues for them to completely freeze back over.

After the tour, the robot always gave Meron a tiny metal box containing a handful of what Rona had begun calling "health pearls." They never figured out why the aliens needed the health pearls, but their effect on humans was incredible: swallowing just a single pearl would make you feel full, healthy, and not at all depressed for a whole week. It was a win-win: the aliens got a heartfelt, personalized tour led by a near-extinct life-form, and Meron and Rona, the last human beings in the universe, got enough health pearls to survive until the next group's visit.

Rona never met the aliens. If it were up to her, she would have joined Meron, but he was adamant, and so every time they landed, she ducked into the hideout they'd set up in the public library's basement. The robot and the tourists were always well behaved, and Meron never felt in any danger, but nevertheless, he thought it would be safer if the aliens believed he was the only person left on Earth and did not find out about Rona. When he gave his spiels about the different sites, he never so much as hinted at her existence, except perhaps when he delivered his monologue about Romeo and Juliet and their overpowering love. Although he didn't mention her by name, he felt Rona's presence in every single word.

Rona died from a rusty nail. The health pearls that offered protection from so many ills turned out to be powerless against tetanus. And so, after surviving a meteorite fall, two hurricanes, one tsunami, and the most catastrophic series of earthquakes ever to hit the planet, Rona ultimately succumbed to a disease for which humans had developed a vaccine more than a century ago.

Meron buried her next to the bench where they'd first kissed, in King David Park. When she got ill, he'd desperately insisted that she take all the health pearls they had left, but now, as he slumped on the bench, he wished he'd kept one for himself. He wasn't sure exactly what he had, but he was burning up with fever and all his muscles ached. "Maybe this is the end," he thought as he lay sweating on the bench near the fresh grave, and shut his eyes. Maybe it was like *Romeo and Juliet*: if he and Rona couldn't live together, at least they would die together.

When he woke up, Meron saw the robot hovering above him, and he could feel a small group of aliens looking at him from behind. He must have been in such a deep sleep that he hadn't heard the spaceship land. He was very weak, but he knew that the only way he could survive was to get more health pearls, and the only way he could do that was to give the tour. He got up and made his way heavily toward the synagogue. The tour took longer than usual, mostly because Meron had to do everything very slowly and he passed out twice. When they finally reached the theater ruins and Meron held out his hand to the robot, instead of placing the cool metal box in Meron's palm, the robot emitted a dissatisfied whistle. Meron shrugged his shoulders uncomprehendingly and kept his hand outstretched. The robot responded with another whistle, this time at a frequency so high that it hurt Meron's ears. He knew that as far as the robot was concerned, the tour wasn't over until Meron told the story of Romeo and Juliet, the pair so in love that they saw no point in living without each other. He sighed and told the story.

Only after the spaceship took off did Meron allow himself to open the metal box and put a pearl in his mouth. His fever broke almost immediately, and by the time he got back to King David Park, his aches and pains had vanished. He looked at the grave. He and Rona had always thought the aliens traveled from the other side of the Milky Way because they wanted to see the Great Synagogue and enjoy a frozen treat on a stick. But that wasn't it. They didn't fly across all those light-years for that. The reason they kept coming back was to hear Meron stand at the ruins of the theater and tell the story of true love and of a race so rare, so sensitive, so unselfish, that it would not hesitate to choose death over heartbreak and loneliness.

OUTSIDE

Three days after the curfew was lifted, it was clear that no one was planning to leave home. After spending so much time indoors, everyone was used to it by now: not going to work, not going to the mall, not meeting a friend for coffee, not getting an unexpected and unwanted hug on the street from someone you took a yoga class with.

The government gave people a few more days to adapt, but when it became obvious that things weren't going to change, they were left with no choice. Police and armed forces began knocking on doors and ordering people to go outside and back to their routines.

After a hundred and twenty days of isolation, it's not always easy to remember what exactly you used to do for a living.

And it's not like you're not trying. It was definitely something involving a lot of angry people who had trouble with authority. A school, perhaps? Or a prison? You have a vague memory of a skinny kid with a mustache throwing a stone at you. Maybe you were a social worker?

You stand on the sidewalk outside your building and the soldiers who walked you out signal for you to start moving. So you do. But you're not sure exactly where you're headed. You scroll through your phone for something that might help you get things straight. Prior appointments, missed calls, addresses in your memos. People rush past you on the street, some looking genuinely panicked. They can't remember where they're supposed to go, either, and if they can, they no longer know how to get there or what exactly to do on the way.

You're dying for a cigarette but you left yours at home. When the soldiers barged in and yelled at you to leave, you barely had time to grab your keys and wallet, even forgetting your sunglasses. You could try to get back inside, but the soldiers are still around, impatiently banging on your neighbors' doors. So you walk to the corner store and find you have nothing but a five-shekel coin in your wallet. The tall young man at the checkout, who reeks of sweat, snatches back the cigarette pack he just handed you: "I'll keep it here for you." When you ask if you can pay with a credit card, he grins like you just told a joke. His hand touched you when he took the cigarettes back, and it was hairy, like a rat. One hundred and twenty days have passed since someone touched you.

Your heart pounds, the air whistles through your lungs, and you're not sure if you're going to make it. Near the ATM sits a man wearing dirty clothes, and there's a tin cup next to him. You do remember what you're supposed to do in this situation. You quickly walk past him and when he tells you in a cracked voice that he hasn't eaten anything in two days, you look in the opposite direction, avoiding eye contact like a pro. There's nothing to be afraid of. It's like riding a bike: the body remembers everything, and the heart that softened while you were alone will harden back up in no time.

A DOG FOR A DOG

For Fida

Yoaz marches several feet ahead of us. He's walking really fast, and Alex and I are half running to keep up with him. Yoaz always walks fast, even faster when he's angry, but I've never seen him like this. In one hand he holds a rusty iron rod we found on the way, and in the other a plastic Sprite bottle that he filled up at the gas station. Alex, out of breath, whispers to me, "He's crazy, your brother. He's seriously crazy."

Yoaz, who must have heard, stops and turns around. "What did you say?" he asks Alex.

"He said we should go to the police," I cut in. "He said let's not get in trouble."

"What's the matter, dork?" Yoaz says, and starts walking toward Alex. "You scared to go into the Arabs' 'hood with us?"

I try to think of something to say. Something that'll make this stop.

When I got home from school, Smadja was already dead. He was lying on the road next to the cemetery, right where our street turns off. At first I thought it was a different dog because his fur looked brown, not white like Smadja's, but when I got closer I realized the brown was dried blood. Alex, who was standing next to the corpse, ran over and told me the whole story: how a silver Renault pickup came speeding over from the Arab side of town and vaulted Smadja up in the air, and how the pickup stopped a few yards down the road and a man with a beard got out. Alex said the man was really tall, with a big white skullcap, the kind Arabs wear; instead of running away, he, Alex, ran toward the pickup yelling, "You killed him! You killed him!" and the Arab, even though he was twice as big as Alex, got scared and quickly hopped back in his truck and drove off.

Me and Alex aren't exactly friends, even though we're the same age and live on the same block. He's probably the only kid in the neighborhood who goes to a different school, and Akiva once told me it's a school for weird kids, where they don't get any homework and everyone has to learn how to knit, even the boys. In the mornings, when Yoaz and I walk to school, we always see Alex waiting for his bus, and he doesn't get home until it's almost dark. Luckily, he threw up that morning, and his thin mom, with the raspy voice and hair like a loofah, decided to keep him home, otherwise he'd never have seen Smadja get run over. "When he drove away, I got my phone out fast and took a picture," Alex said, and proudly showed me a blurry image of a license plate. "See? When the police have this number, they'll catch him in a second."

Yoaz and I dug a grave for Smadja on the hill next to the cemetery. Yoaz said it was okay according to Jewish law, and that it was the best thing for Smadja, because he wouldn't be buried alone. Alex wanted to help dig, but Yoaz hogged the shovel and said digging calmed him down, and he wouldn't let anyone else do it except me. After we lowered Smadja into the pit, Yoaz said I could say a few words—like, not exactly a prayer, because he's a dog, but just something about him. So I said that he was a good dog, and that when I got him for my ninth birthday, when he was a puppy, there was a story on TV about Oren Smadja, who'd won a bronze medal at the Olympics, and they showed him on the mat doing judo rolls, and he looked exactly like a puppy rolling, and that's when I named him Smadja, and Yoaz and Dad didn't think it was a great name for a dog, but Mom said it was my decision—here Yoaz cut me off and said I didn't have to bring up every single thing that happened since he was born, but to just say something about him from my heart, like how even when I'm a hundred and something years old I'll still remember him. Or, he said, I could swear an oath over his grave.

"An oath?" Alex intervened. "Like what kind of oath?" Yoaz said I could swear that if I ever had another dog, I'd name him Smadja, in the first Smadja's memory, or I could swear to avenge his death. And when Yoaz said that, Alex took his phone out and said, "Telling the police isn't taking revenge . . ."

Yoaz snorted. "Who said anything about the police?" He started covering up the grave. "Me and Nadav'll take care of it ourselves."

"I'm telling you," Alex continued, "with my picture of the plates, they'll get him in no time. . . ."

"'They'll get him in no time. . . .'" Yoaz mimicked Alex's squeaky voice. "Who? Who's gonna get him, you dork? Your knitting teacher at the girls' school?"

"It's not a girls' school, it's a Waldorf school! And if Nadav files a complaint, then the Israel Police—"

"The Israel Police?" Yoaz interrupted. "The Israel Police can't even arrest people murderers. You really think they give a shit about a dog murderer?"

"But if we don't go to the police, what exactly are we supposed to do?" Alex sounded frightened now.

Yoaz kept piling dirt over the grave, and when he finished, he tossed the shovel aside, looked at me, and said, "Come on, dude, we're going to the Arabs' 'hood."

Yoaz and I start walking. Alex joins in but stays a few steps behind us, so as not to irritate Yoaz. "Hey," I say to Yoaz, mostly to try to calm him down, "what did you put in the bottle? Kerosene?"

"Gasoline," Yoaz says, and pulls a plastic orange lighter out of his pocket. "Let's do this." He flicks the lighter on and holds it close to me. "Bonfire night! Who's coming with me to burn an Arab's dog?"

"Wait!" Alex says, grabbing my arm with his freckled hands. "Wait! Think for a second! It doesn't make any sense to go kill some dog we don't even know, who has nothing to do with—"

"It doesn't make sense?" Yoaz puts his angry face right in Alex's. "It's what the Bible says. Are you telling me the Bible doesn't make sense, either?"

"It doesn't say anywhere in the Bible that if someone runs over your—"

But Yoaz won't let him finish. "An eye for an eye!" he yells. "A tooth for a tooth! That's in Exodus. Don't they teach you anything at your lousy school?"

"Come on, Yoaz, there's no comparison. That pickup driver—"

"The Arab," Yoaz snaps. "Say 'Arab.'"

"Okay," Alex says. "Okay, the Arab. I saw it happen. He really did bail and that was an asshole thing to do. But he didn't do it on purpose."

"No shit?" Yoaz winks at me and looks at Alex. "Trust me, when we burn one of their dogs today, it also won't be on purpose."

Alex takes his phone out and waves it around in Yoaz's face. "You're messed up!" he yells. "If you and Nadav don't throw away that bottle and lighter right now and go back home, I'm calling the police and telling them everything."

Yoaz slaps Alex with the hand that's not holding the Sprite bottle. It's his weak hand, but it's enough to knock Alex's phone to the ground, and Alex starts crying. Yoaz picks up the phone and puts it in his own pocket. "You're not hearing what I'm saying: No police. Just us. Now, go home, and I swear, if you even say one word . . ."

"My phone . . ." Alex whimpers, holding out his hand. "My phone . . ."

"Later," Yoaz barks. "If you watch your mouth, Nadav'll give it to you later, when we get back." He turns around and keeps marching toward the train tracks, and I have to practically run to keep up.

"Nadav!" Alex shouts behind me. "Don't go with him! He's a psycho!" But Yoaz doesn't even turn around to see if I'm coming. He knows I'm behind him.

In the Arabs' neighborhood, there's hardly a single streetlamp. Yoaz knows it well. He and his friends sometimes go there after school to eat hummus. We have hummus in our neighborhood, too, but Yoaz says the Arabs' hummus tastes better and costs half the price. He leads us through a narrow, half-hidden walkway into an empty lot covered with trash, and next to it is some kind of storage building with a fence. Even before we get near it, I can hear a dog barking, and a second later we see a giant, angry-looking Doberman. Yoaz says it's a shoe warehouse, and once the Arabs who work there threatened a kid from his class who pissed on the fence and said they'd sic the dog on him. "We're gonna have ourselves a barbecue tonight," he says, and takes out a piece of salami he'd been keeping in his pocket. "Tonight we're gonna teach them that a Jewish dog's blood is not cheap."

Yoaz has a simple plan. All I have to do is take the salami, hold it up to a gap in the fence, and call the dog over. When the dog smells the meat and comes closer, Yoaz will douse him with gas from the bottle and light it up.

"I don't want to," I tell him.

Yoaz sighs. "What do you mean you don't want to? Then what did we come all the way here for? Go on, take it!" He shoves the salami wrapped in paper into my hand.

"Look at him." I point at the dog, who's on the other side of the fence, playing with a shoebox. "He's just a poor dog."

"A poor dog?" Yoaz snaps. "What's so poor about him?

You think he's like Smadja? You think you can throw him a ball and he'll fetch? If this fence wasn't here, he'd have ripped you to shreds by now." I stand silently holding the salami, and Yoaz comes closer and puts his hand on my shoulder. "Come on, Nadav," he says softly, "let's get it over with." Then he whispers, "Do it for Smadja."

"I don't want to burn him."

"I don't, either. Believe me, I don't. But if we don't do it, if we don't teach them a lesson, once and for all, it'll never end. Smadja was only your first dog. Do you want them to run over the next one, too?" When I don't answer, he goes on, "Come on, it's on me. You don't have to do anything. Just give him the salami. I'd do it myself, but I need both hands to pour the gas and light it." I shake my head. "I don't understand you," Yoaz says, putting his face right up to mine. "I don't understand. Do you have any idea what it's like when your dog dies? Every night you're going to dream about him. Every night he's going to come to you in your dreams, run over, with tire marks on his belly, and he's going to look at you with the saddest eyes and howl. And when he does, what then? Are you also going to shake your head like a little baby? Gimme that!" He grabs the salami. "Never mind, you spoiled brat. I'll do it on my own."

Yoaz twists the cap off the bottle and flicks it onto the ground. He unwraps the salami, holds it in his teeth, and walks over to the fence. He tries to call the dog, but with the salami in his mouth you can't understand what he's saying. About twenty feet away, the Arabs' dog keeps playing with the shoebox, which by now is in shreds, and completely ignores Yoaz's calls. After a minute, Yoaz comes back to me. "Nadav," he says in the most pleading voice I've ever heard him use, "I can't do it alone, I need you. Help me!" I try to say something but my words get mixed up, and when I start crying, Yoaz hugs me, and his hug smells like gasoline and meat. In the middle of the hug, Alex's phone rings. Yoaz lets go, puts the lighter back in his pocket, pulls out the phone, and looks at the screen. "It's his kooky mom," he hisses.

"That narc," I say. "I bet he told her everything."

Before we go home, we chuck the lighter and the bottle of gasoline in a dumpster. That way, if Alex's mom calls our dad and tells him what we were doing, there won't be any evidence. I feed the salami to the Arabs' dog through the fence, and he chows down on it. It's good salami. Mom always puts it in my sandwiches with mayonnaise and pickles. It would be a pity to throw that away.

PRESENT PERFECT

t's about time we acknowledge it: people are not very good at remembering things the way they really happened. If an experience is an article of clothing, then memory is the garment after it's been washed, not according to the instructions, over and over again: the colors fade, the size shrinks, the original, nostalgic scent has long since become the artificial orchid smell of fabric softener.

Giora Shviro, may he rest in peace, was thinking all this while standing in line to get into the next world. The line looked long, almost endless, but somehow time flowed differently in it and the waiting was a lot more bearable than it was, let's say, in an airport security line or at a doctor's office, situations that Giora, who always flew first-class and was treated in prestigious clinics, wasn't familiar with anyway. But in that particular line, there didn't seem to be any short-cuts. Everyone appeared to be equal in the face of death, or in the face of the Creator or whoever it was waiting for them way up there at the head of the endless line. Although, who knows, Giora thought, maybe there's another entrance for virtuous men that he and the others didn't know about. The more he thought about it, the more likely it seemed that there had to be a secret VIP entrance. After all, it doesn't seem reasonable that when the Virgin Mary or Mahatma Gandhi died, they had to stand in line like everyone else.

But don't get me wrong, it isn't that the line didn't move. It did, the whole time, except that even now, after Giora had been waiting in it for . . . for . . . So that's just it, when we said that time in that line behaved differently, we actually meant to say that it didn't really exist. I mean, it did exist, because time always has to exist, but it's just that somehow, Giora and the others couldn't seem to estimate or measure it. The tall woman with the bindi on her forehead standing in front of Giora explained to him that it was like Nirvana, and the old guy with bad breath standing behind him claimed it was a little like dementia, but in a good way. "Interesting," Giora thought, "what could be good about dementia? Maybe it's the fact that dementia makes you forget a life you'd rather not remember, anyway?" But even that thought faded in his mind before he could finish thinking it, and an instant before another aimless thought replaced it, he caught sight of the white wing of an angel.

The angel was standing in line, too, about twenty people ahead of him, waiting patiently like everyone else. From that distance, it seemed to Giora as if he were swaying in place and talking to himself, and maybe he was even praying, although why would an angel waiting in line to get into the next world be praying? That whole praying thing is totally normal in the world of the living, but after death, you would expect an angel in heaven to communicate with the Creator in a slightly more direct, reliable way. "That needs to be checked out," Giora thought. When he was still alive, he was an analyst in a successful hedge fund, and the first thing they taught him when he started working there was that if one of the managers makes a mistake or just asks Giora to do something that doesn't sit right with him, instead of disagreeing or arguing, it's better to say, "That needs to be checked out," and wait patiently until the whole thing blows over. But this time, it wasn't a polite brush-off, this time it was about an issue Giora was truly invested in, and he really felt he had to check it out.

The tall woman with the bindi and the old guy with bad breath promised Giora that, while he went to question the angel, they would save his place in line, and that promise was enough to enable Giora to work up his courage and go for it.

"Excuse me!" he said to the angel, who at first ignored

him. "Excuse me! Yes, you. Can I ask you a question?" The angel, who seemed a bit distant, nodded. "Thank you," Giora said, giving a forced bow. "It's just that maybe you could give me a quick description of this whole next-world operation, you being an angel and all? Territorial boundaries, hierarchal structures, you know, all the important stuff."

The angel tried to evade his questions, claiming he wasn't an angel, he just happened to have wings, but angels aren't great liars, at least not for an extended period of time, and it took . . . it took . . . Okay, we already mentioned the strange way time passes here, so Giora couldn't really say how long it took, but at some point, the angel admitted he was an angel and explained to Giora in a whisper that his job was to mingle with the dead to make sure everything was running smoothly and there were no problems.

"And if you do come up against a problem?" Giora asked. "What exactly are you supposed to do? Is there a protocol? Do you have to report it to someone? Take care of it yourself?"

The angel thought for a moment and then began stammering. The truth is that, as an angel, he had never come across a problem. After all, dead people congregate in an orderly way, so what could happen? He did remember that, during the briefing, they told him what to do if there were disruptions, but that was so long ago, he didn't remember what it was.

The pale woman standing behind the angel told Giora

that he was being noisy and it was very annoying. You could tell she suspected that Giora's whole conversation with the angel was just an excuse to get ahead of her in line. Giora apologized immediately and explained that he was just checking out some small technical thing and the second he finished, he'd go right back to his place in line. The truth is, he no longer remembered where his place in line was. He remembered a man or woman who was tall or old or had bad breath . . . or a bindi . . . and meanwhile, the angel managed to forget what Giora had asked him, and Giora himself, who also forgot what he'd asked earlier, now asked, "Tell me, with all this Divine Spirit and omnipotence and everything, couldn't you set up a more efficient operation? You know, something without a line."

The angel gave Giora a confused look. "Line?" he asked. "What exactly do you mean?"

"What do I mean?" Giora sneered. "I mean you and me and all these people who have been waiting here with us . . . for . . . I don't know, a long time. You know, all . . . this." Giora made a limp gesture with his hands that was meant to take in all the people standing in front of them and behind them, waiting quietly.

"This?" the angel asked, shrugging his wings. "This, if I understand correctly, is heaven."

DIRECTOR'S CUT

For Jess

Maček Smolansky was a filmmaker, entrepreneur, and philosopher. But above all, he was a perfectionist. Which is why no one was particularly surprised when he announced that his new film, titled *Life*, would be shot on three cameras and would correspond, minute to minute, with a human lifespan. Filming began at the birth of Pavel Krotoczowski, the introverted protagonist, and lasted seventy-three years. On the set of the final scene, in which Pavel hangs himself in his basement after being diagnosed with late-stage prostate cancer, the entire crew wept. Even the soundman's desperate shushing could not stop the tears.

Post-production took a hundred and fourteen years. Maček died of old age a few months after it started. Sound editing continued for another ninety-six years, and on social media there were several complaints that it was sloppily done.

All the leading film critics were invited to the premiere, and the few tickets offered to the public were sold on the black market at exorbitant prices. The film, as promised, was seventy-three years long. When the closing credits rolled and the lights came on, the ushers discovered that the audience was dead. Most of it was giving off a pretty good stench. But among all these decaying corpses sat one lone surviving viewer, naked and balding, and sobbing like a baby. When his tears dried, he wiped his eyes, stood up, and calmly walked up the aisle.

This aging man was the son of a famous film critic who hadn't even known she was pregnant when she sat down to watch the film. He was born eight months into the screening and grew up in the dark cinema, transfixed by the screen. When he opened the doors and stepped out into the street, he was blinded by the sun. The dozens of reporters waiting outside the theater shoved microphones at him and asked what he thought of the movie. "Movie?" stammered the bald man as he blinked at the sunlight. All along, he'd thought it was life.

GRAVITY

Three days after they moved into their new apartment, the woman who lived upstairs jumped out of her window. Romi was walking back from the coffee shop, carrying two lattes, just as the woman from the eighth floor hit the sidewalk. Romi dropped the drink carrier, spilling coffee all over herself, and her eyes locked in on the stains on her sweatpants so that she wouldn't have to see anything else. She heard running, panting, and talking, and within seconds there were almost twenty people there, and the guy with the unibrow who cleaned the lobby was calling an ambulance. Someone said the woman's name was Rinat or Ronit, and someone else said she'd seen her crying in the elevator a few days earlier. "It's because of Covid," the cleaner said. "Everyone's committing suicide these days. They were just talking about it on the news."

The distant siren mingled with the vibration of Romi's phone. It was Daniel, but she didn't want to tell him everything over the phone. She touched her cheeks to make sure she wasn't crying, took a deep breath, and kept walking up to the building. "Hey!" she heard the cleaner calling after her. When she turned around, he yelled, "Lady, where d'you think you're going? You're a witness."

"A witness to what?" Romi asked. "I didn't see anything."

But the cleaner wouldn't back down. "You were the closest one!" he shouted. "Look—her blood's all over your clothes!"

"It's not blood. It's coffee. I dropped my coffee," Romi said.

"Well, it looks like blood to me," the cleaner proclaimed. "The police should have a look at it." Romi froze for a moment, but when her phone started vibrating again, she kept walking.

"Hey!" the cleaner yelled again, but then a different male voice said, "Forget it. Poor girl, leave her alone."

Daniel opened the door irritably. "You're screening my calls?" he asked, but before she could explain, he saw the stains on her sweats and said, "What's going on? Are you okay?" Romi wanted to tell him about the neighbor who'd jumped and about the unibrow cleaner and about how the stains on her pants would probably never come out, but all she could manage was a strange whimper, and Daniel quickly came over and gave her one of his feeble hugs that barely touched. "Stop, baby, what's the matter?"

She told him everything. She wanted to feel sorry for the neighbor and say how horrible it was and how she must have really been suffering, but all that came out was anger. They'd plunked down 3.4 million shekels for this apartment. Daniel's mother had given them almost a million and a half, and they'd taken out a twenty-three-year mortgage for the rest. Twenty-three years! If Daniel got her pregnant now with post-traumatic sex and they had a boy, she thought, the kid would grow up, finish high school, join the army, fight a war, and be discharged—and she and Daniel would still be paying for the apartment every month. And every time he came home from kindergarten—this kid who didn't even exist yet—or from school, or on leave from the army, he would step over the spot where that Rinat or Ronit woman's body now lay.

This neighborhood had been purpose-built for "upwardly mobile young professionals." People who bought homes here wanted to improve their lives: they took out loans; they poured in blood, sweat, and tears; and for what? So that some Rinat or Ronit could jump out her window and crush the life out of them? Even if a woman was depressed, she could at least grasp that she's not the only person in this world and have the decency to kill herself in bed or in the bathroom instead of plunging onto her neighbor's head. "I don't want this," Romi told Daniel. "I don't want to live here anymore. I can't live in a building where people jump."

"Calm down, babe," Daniel said, and tried to stroke her. "It's not the building. It's one woman who jumped. Poor thing. It has nothing to do with us at all."

"She's not a poor thing," Romi fumed. "I'm the poor thing! Me and you and your mom. For *this* she dipped into her pension? So some neighbor whose name we don't even know could commit suicide right on our heads?"

The woman's name turned out to be Sarit, and the next day Daniel made them go to the funeral. He said they needed closure, and that as far as he was concerned, it was either a funeral or couples therapy. Romi had no desire to go to the funeral, but therapy sounded even worse, like a cross between mud wrestling and divorce court. Daniel typed the cemetery's address into Waze, and they hardly spoke the whole way. When they arrived, he insisted on buying flowers from some religious guy who was selling half-wilted bunches out of black buckets. There were maybe ten other people there, and the only one she recognized was the cleaner from the lobby, who hurried over and said it was totally unacceptable that she'd left before the police got there yesterday. Instead of standing by her and telling the cleaner to leave her alone, Daniel nodded and said, "You're right, you're right," and the cleaner walked away and came back a minute later with an elderly couple whose eyes were puffy. "See?" he said, gesturing at Romi. "This is the neighbor I told you about, who saw your daughter fall." The elderly man nodded and held out his hand, and even though Romi and Daniel were very strict about social distancing, they both shook his hand. "I'm Pinchas," he said, "and this is Tzippora." After a moment, perhaps because no one said anything, he added, "We're Sarit's parents," and as soon as he said that, Tzippora started crying. "When she fell," Pinchas asked Romi, "could you see her? Her face?" Romi didn't answer. She didn't know what to say and she hoped that if she waited long enough, Daniel would say something to get her out of it. But he kept quiet, and they all stood in silence, except for the mother, who was weeping.

That night, Daniel fell asleep instantly and started snoring. Romi lay awake in bed for almost an hour and then got up, rolled a joint, and went out onto the balcony. A friend of Daniel's had sold them the pot; it smelled like cookies and was really potent. Romi looked down over the railing and tried to find the spot where that Sarit woman had hit the ground. At the funeral, the cleaner had talked about how the gray sidewalk had been covered with blood, but now, from seven floors up, everything looked clean and fresh, and a young couple were standing there making out.

When Romi had told Daniel that she was angry at that woman for deciding to kill herself right on her, Daniel said she was self-centered and it was time she understood that not everything in the world had to do with her. But as she watched the couple practically fucking on the neatly trimmed hedge in front of her building, she couldn't stop thinking that maybe it did have something to do with her. And that maybe Sarit had once believed that the new smell coming from the walls and the gleaming white marble in the lobby would re-start her life, and then, when she'd looked out and seen Romi coming back from the coffee shop in her sweats, she'd had the impression, from that high-up vantage point, that Romi was happy and had a perfect marriage, just like the two pa-per cups in her coffee carrier. And Sarit just couldn't take it anymore, so she'd jumped out the window to ruin everything for Romi. Much like Romi was dying to plummet onto those noisy lovers moaning down there and knock the lust out of them.

CHINESE SINGLES DAY

A few weeks ago, my wife finds an online store selling the dining table set she's been talking about for months, at $180 less than what it costs in Israel. The regular price at this store is much higher, but in honor of Chinese Singles Day, it's on sale for 30 percent off, and they're throwing in a free baby seat. To me, the whole thing doesn't sound kosher. Why would a Chinese single want a baby seat? My wife says I don't know the first thing about marketing: the sale is in honor of Singles Day—it's not a sale *for* singles. I still think it's fishy. Kind of like giving out free hamburgers on World Vegan Day. "It's not the same thing at all," my wife insists. "Vegans are against killing animals, but singles have nothing against babies." She's very good at arguing, my wife.

On our honeymoon, we saw a seal dozing on the beach from the deck of our cruise ship, and it took her less than five minutes to convince me that I was confused and it was just an old tire.

"Okay," I concede, "forget the Chinese for a second. What exactly are we supposed to do with a baby seat? We don't have kids."

"You never know. . . . Besides, even if we throw it in the trash, we're still saving a hundred eighty dollars."

For the two weeks while the dining set is being shipped, we don't fight even once, and we also do not find a baby under a toadstool. When the set arrives, we invite some friends over for a fancy dinner. These friends are a couple we're not all that close with, but they have a baby. The baby's name is Netzach, which means "eternity," because his parents are very ambitious and they like to think big. Netzach cries and screams all evening. After dinner, I tell the friends how we got the baby seat as a freebie with the dining set, and I ask if they'd like it. The woman hesitates: "Are you sure? What if you need it?" My wife reassures her that there's no chance of that happening because I'm sterile. Backing her up, I let the couple in on how my wife refuses to adopt a baby because she's afraid it'll grow up dumb or ugly. "Adopting isn't like natural birth," I explain, "when the baby comes out, you know . . . like you." The friends still seem tentative, but eventually they take the baby seat, and the baby, who hasn't stopped whining and drooling for a second.

That night, I dream that we order a Chinese baby on the internet and the delivery guy drops her off at our doorstep, swaddled in Bubble Wrap. The baby in my dream is very cute, and when she looks at me, she keeps murmuring a word I can't understand, like a mantra. My wife claims she's saying "Daddy" in Chinese, but when I look it up on Google Translate, I discover that what our baby is saying over and over is the Chinese word for "customer." "She looks just like you," I tell my wife in the dream. She doesn't: she's Chinese. I'm just trying to be nice.

INSOMNIA

Three a.m. is prime time for the soul. Programming should start any minute, and it's hard to tell what'll be on this time, so is it any wonder you're breaking into a sweat? Sometimes they broadcast anxiety, on weekends it's depression, and then there's the big hit—that feeling that makes your whole body tremble and your throat close up. It's not happiness. If it were happiness, you would know. You've read enough about happiness to know that it shouldn't be anywhere near this painful.

In bed next to you, a beautiful woman with her mouth open draws a perfect circle of saliva on the pillow. You love her forever but you know she'll die in the end. You'll die, too, and with any luck it'll be a minute or two before she does.

You've never been good at mourning, at tears, at nodding understandingly to visitors who come to console. In the other room, a curious boy who has yet to learn what fear is snores like an old man sawing off the tree trunk of his life. A woman and a child sleep close to you, as selfish and angry as everyone else on the block, but they're yours. Yours not like property that is bought or taken or plundered. Yours like weeds that spring up inside you from the bottom of your soul, poking through the cracks without any plan or purpose. They're not there to beautify or glorify or perfume the air with their blossoms. They're not there. They're here.

You shut your eyes, your lids bowing gratefully to the gods of sleep. Four hours from now, if the sun comes up, you'll wake again to a magnificent morning erection. It's pretty amazing that someone your age still gets up every day with such a fierce urge to fuck the world.

ZEN FOR BEGINNERS

For Tamara

At the end of his private yoga class, when Gavri paid the teacher, instead of thanking him or chirping, "See you next week!" she gave him a penetrating look and said, "You have to learn how to let go." Gavri nodded without answering. He found it irritating that she would say something like that, out of nowhere. She was his yoga teacher, not his therapist or his guru or whatever it was called, and he went to her classes to make his back hurt less. That's all. That's as far as it went. This teacher, Lital, was a little chubby, but Gavri would never have dreamed of telling her, "You really should lay off the junk food," would he? "People sometimes don't know their place," he thought as he walked up the stairs in his apartment building, but when he got to the third floor, something else started bothering him. On the right side of the landing, where his apartment door should have been, was the neighbor Stella's brown wooden door with the sign saying THE KIRSCHNERS, while his own familiar white door, with their names and the boat that Omri had drawn at pre-school, was now on the left side. Gavri tentatively put his key in the lock and the door opened right up.

Omri and Mirit were in the living room, humming along with a kids' song. Omri ran over, shouting, "Daddy! We had a Lego contest today and I won!" "My talented little boy," Gavri said, mussing Omri's hair, and then he whispered to Mirit, "Hey, what's the deal with the door?" Mirit had no idea what he was talking about. "It's on the left side," he explained, and when she gave him a questioning look, he became a little im-patient. "Don't you remember that our apartment door was on the right?" "No," Mirit said with an apologetic smile, "but you know me, I have a terrible sense of direction . . ." "Mirit," Gavri said, trying to sound dramatic, "look at me. The door was definitely on the other side of the landing. Do you believe me?" "I believe you," Mirit said, and she laughed, but it was a slightly anxious laugh: "I totally believe you. But why are you making such a big deal out of it? Does it really matter which side of the building we're on?"

That evening, Gavri ran into Stella on the landing, and when he asked if she happened to remember which side her apartment had been on that morning, she looked at him as if he'd lost his mind. Thinking about it at night as he lay in bed with his eyes open, he decided it really wasn't such a big deal. And real estate–wise, they'd come out ahead, because now they had a rear-facing apartment, which was worth even more. Still, he had trouble falling asleep.

At his next yoga class, he tried to engage the teacher in small talk. He told her that, thanks to the class, he'd started reading about Buddhism and he found it very interesting. Lital nodded and recalled that someone at her teacher training had said it was related, but she was more into the physical side of yoga and she hadn't had the chance to delve into all that stuff. When he got home after class, he had trouble finding their building. It was strange, because all these years it had been right next to the 15 bus stop, and now all of a sudden it was on the other side of the street. Omri was waiting for him in the living room, wearing a new pirate costume that Mirit had bought for Purim. "So, what do you think about our little pirate son!" Mirit exclaimed. Omri waved his plastic sword around: "Argh! Give me all your treasure or I'll feed you to the sharks!" "Adorable," said Gavri, "adorable. I just have to ask, honey: did you notice that . . . our building moved?" Mirit gave him a worried look and whispered, "My love, please don't start that again. Stella told me you asked her about this business with the . . . shifting. It made her very anxious, and you know she's not all that young or healthy anymore—" "No, no," Gavri interrupted, "it's not about the apartment. It's just that our whole building . . . well, it used to be east of the square, and now it's on the other side. Didn't you notice when you came back from preschool?" "No," Mirit admitted, "I didn't. Why? Is this side not as good?"

The following week after yoga, he was tense the whole way home. The building hadn't moved this time, but Gavri discovered that their apartment was now on the fourth floor. He was about to bring it up with Mirit, but he decided to drop it. He stepped out onto the balcony. Now that they'd switched sides and climbed one floor higher, they had a view of the sea. Mirit followed him outside and handed him a glass of Diet Coke, and they sat quietly gazing at the red sun setting over the water. "What are you thinking about, my love?" she asked, and stroked his face. "Nothing," Gavri said with a smile, and put his hand on her shoulder, "just something my yoga teacher told me a while ago." "Want another Coke?" Mirit asked. "Or something to nibble?" "No, thanks," Gavri said, "I have everything I need."

SQUIRRELS

For Danna and Omri

When Tom's grandfather realized he wasn't going to survive his smoker's cancer, he convened the whole family and informed them that as soon as he died, he was planning to be reincarnated in a different body and come back to Grandma. "I love you all," he told the relatives gathered around his bed, "but to tell you the truth, one incarnation with you is plenty. I'm ready to say goodbye and move on. But you"—he cupped the wrinkled hand of Tom's grandmother, who was sitting at his bedside—"you are my eternal beloved and we will always be together."

Tom's grandfather believed in reincarnation. He had this theory that when the soul departs the body, it forgets almost everything, and that's why, when you get near death, you have to train the soul to remember two things: one person and one place it wants to return to. When it came to the person, Tom's grandfather didn't have to do any training: he thought about his wife all the time, anyway. As for the place, he told anyone who would listen, over and over, that when he came back in the next life, he would wait for Tom's grandmother on the red bench outside the radiology clinic at the hospital. That was the bench where they used to sit together, chain-smoking, while they waited for his radiation treatment. If a doctor walked past and dared to throw out a comment about how he shouldn't be smoking in his state, Tom's grandfather would wink at Grandma and say, "And if I do keep smoking, Doctor? What's the worst that could happen? I'll get even more cancer?"

After Tom's grandfather died, Tom's grandmother visited the red bench at the hospital every week and sat there waiting for Tom's grandfather to arrive in his new body. But he never did. Within a few months, she stopped going, and a couple of years later she moved into a retirement home. There she met a widower named Chester, and an affair of sorts blossomed. Chester, who was almost eighty, wanted to get married. Tom's grandmother wasn't thrilled at the idea, but Chester was very persistent and eventually she agreed, on the condition that they held the ceremony next to the red bench, in homage to Tom's grandfather.

At the wedding, there were fewer than a dozen people,

including the priest and Tom, who had just graduated from high school but hadn't yet left for college. The ceremony was traditional, a little boring even, until the moment when the priest asked Chester if he would take Tom's grandmother to be his wife. Before the excited groom could answer, a giant squirrel appeared out of nowhere and bit his hand. The startled Chester shrieked in pain, and the priest, who made a very un-Christian attempt to kick the elusive squirrel, lost his balance and fell on his back. Within seconds, the wedding had descended into chaos. It took almost an hour to tend to Chester and the priest and calm them down, and as soon as the injured priest resumed the ceremony, the squirrel dropped from a treetop and tried to attack poor Chester again. This time he wasn't able to hurt anyone, but Tom's grandmother had had enough. She announced that the wedding was off and she was leaving Chester.

She lived in the retirement home until the day she died. Twice a week, Tom picked her up in his parents' car and drove her to the red bench at the hospital, where she waited for the giant squirrel. The squirrel didn't always turn up, but when he did, he jumped on her lap and curled up like a baby, and they would sit there for hours without saying a word.

Tom told this story to Naomi on their first date. They were at a mediocre Italian restaurant in Urbana, Illinois, and Naomi, who hadn't been all that excited in the first place about going on a blind date with her coworker's brother who wrote a blog

about global warming, asked herself what it said about Tom
if the first thing he told her on a date was that his grandfather was a violent, jealous squirrel. When Tom took her
home, she told him he was cute but she had trouble imagin-
ing the two of them together. Tom laughed and said, "You
don't have to imagine it. Here we are. Together. And if you go
out with me tomorrow, we'll be together again, without your
having to imagine anything." "No," said Naomi, "I meant that
I can't imagine us . . . you know . . . as a couple." After an awkward silence, Tom said, "Okay. Then let's not try to imagine
ourselves as a couple and settle for something more modest:
you and me in my apartment, eating bibimbap that I cooked
from my Korean roommate's grandmother's secret recipe."

The next day, he really did make her the best meal she'd
ever had in her life, and he showed her his crazy collection of
old greeting cards, and they sat talking until three a.m.

They married within the year, and a few months later Naomi got pregnant. They hadn't even been thinking about
kids, and when it happened, they felt as if someone had given
them an enormous, surprising gift. The kind that takes nine
months to unwrap.

Naomi started buying all the things they were going to
need for the baby hiding in her belly, and Tom took his toolbox out of the shed and began building an oak cradle, which
they planned to paint sky blue. One evening, when she got
home from work, Naomi found Tom passed out next to the

cradle. By the time the ambulance arrived, he'd regained consciousness, and at the hospital, after a series of tests, Tom was diagnosed with a brain tumor. If they'd found it only a few months earlier, it could have been treated.

Naomi cried all night, while Tom, who was strangely calm, tried to comfort her and said she was the best thing that had ever happened to him, and that even though he would like to live with her for another eighty years, he wasn't greedy and he was grateful for all the happiness he'd shared with her these past eighteen months. "But I *am* greedy," Naomi wept, "and I'm not willing to give you up, do you hear me? I won't let you die and leave me on my own with a baby and a pile of broken dreams."

The doctors said Tom had three months to live, at most. He would die before their child was born and there was nothing in the world they could do about it. But Naomi had an idea. She dragged the almost-finished cradle into their bedroom and told Tom that from now until he left this world, she wanted him to look at that cradle and remember it. He had to memorize the cradle and her. Just like his grandfather had remembered that bench outside the hospital and Tom's grandmother. "You'll remember, and after you die you'll come back," she said in a trembling voice, "just like him. You'll come back and we'll be together forever." Tom nodded, and when she leaned in to hug him, she could see how sad he was. It was the only time Naomi had seen him that sad.

Tom Jr. was born two weeks after his father died. He had Naomi's almond-shaped green eyes, but his smile was definitely his father's. And when he smiled, Naomi couldn't help feeling that Tom had never left, that he was simply there with them. But then things started getting weird. Every time she nursed Tom Jr., he would look up at her, not the way a baby looks at its mother but the way a man looks at a woman's bared breast. His gaze and the touch of his lips confused her, and it all got very distressing and made Naomi hate herself and feel guilty. It's perverse to be the mother of a baby who is sometimes a child and sometimes the love of your life, and Naomi felt she was starting to lose her grip.

When she told all this to Tom's older sister, she gave Naomi a bemused look. "All this to-do," she said, "all this craziness, just because of that stupid story about Granddad and the squirrel?" Tom's sister said she knew the story and that she'd been there when the squirrel had bitten Chester, but it wasn't her grandfather, just a fat, angry squirrel. She said the only reason the wedding was called off was because her grandmother hadn't really loved Chester and she thought he was kind of whiny. Everything else was just folklore and excuses. "You have to let it go," she told Naomi. "Tom is dead, and you have a whole life to live: a child to raise, men to meet, new places to visit. You're still young and curious and vivacious; don't bury yourself with him."

AUTOCORRECT

That same day, Naomi bought Tom Jr. a cheap plastic cradle at Walmart. She locked the wooden one in the shed, and that helped. Very slowly, she released all those ludicrous ideas about Tom's soul being reincarnated in Tom Jr., and in return she gained a lovable, sweet boy. After a few months she even downloaded Tinder. She never used it, but the fact that it was there on her phone promised that she might find love in the future.

The first guy Naomi went out with after Tom died was named Sasha. He hit on her in the line for the ATM, and even though he was covered with tattoos and didn't look like her type, she gave him her phone number. Because he was funny, and also because she remembered thinking that Tom wasn't her type, either, the first time they'd met. She and Sasha took things slowly, which was perfect for Naomi. He was a tattoo artist who worked crazy hours all week, and they mostly saw each other on weekends. He taught Tom Jr. how to draw, and they would spend hours sitting in the kitchen together sketching robots and dragons. When Naomi's birthday was coming up, Sasha offered to ink her a tattoo as a gift. At first she refused. She said that anything she decided she liked and wanted now, she would inevitably regret in a year. But Sasha wouldn't give up, and Tom Jr. said, "Think carefully, Mom. There must be something Sasha could tattoo that you'll always love: ice cream, a skateboard, a hot dog with lots of mustard."

"Fortunately," Sasha said with a grin, "I happen to be the number-one hot dog tattooer in the country."

Naomi laughed and said she wasn't that keen on hot dogs, but there had to be something else. She'd think about it. Maybe a squirrel. "You're in luck," said Sasha, "I'm good at squirrels, too."

LIFE: SPOILER ALERT

Living is the easiest thing in the world. Your mom pushes, a man in a white coat on the other side of the uterus pulls. Out you pop, and someone cuts your umbilical cord. You start crying. The lights are too bright. Air enters your lungs. Air exits your lungs. Air enters your lungs. Air exits. Air enters. Exits. It's a piece of cake. A walk in the park. You're alive.

Living is the easiest thing in the world. Surviving . . . that's another story. They attack you with pitchforks, they attack you with batons. They attack you with axes, with diseases, with cars. They come at you with tsunamis, with earthquakes, with a stroke. With a malignant tumor, a benign tumor, malignant tumor, benign tumor, malignant tumor. Let's see you get out of that alive.

And if you've somehow managed to survive this far, now is the time to step things up and try to start caring: about a cat wailing in the yard, a baby wailing on the neighbor's balcony, a homeless guy wailing on the sidewalk across the street. I know, it's not easy. Surviving is intuitive: a bear chases you, you run. But caring? That's for advanced players. Breaking up a fight between two strangers on the street. Giving the salami sandwich you packed for lunch to a hungry-looking guy with holes in his shirt. Remembering that salami is actually thick slices of a cow that didn't ask to die. Understanding that you're part of something bigger, part of a giant, bloodied human wound. That this disease called caring is incurable and always will be.

Death is a fact. The only questions are when and how: in the crib, by drowning, from a mysterious virus, on the way home from a bar, drunk, in a crash merging onto the highway. It comes and it's almost surprising how predictable it is. It comes and then immediately—quiet.

A HYPOTHETICAL QUESTION

For beloved Nurit

I f we were shipwrecked on a desert island and had nothing to eat, and you died," said the man lying naked in bed, "I would never—and I mean *never*—eat you. I would lie there next to your body, grief-stricken and starving, for days, and the thought wouldn't even cross my mind."

"Well, I'd eat you, and I'd do it quick," said the woman, planting a kiss on him. "I'd do it while your body was still warm, before the meat could spoil."

"What?" The man moved away from her and sat up in bed. "Are you serious? How can you even say something like that? What sort of a person could eat the flesh . . . the quivering heart that never stopped loving her even for a moment?"

"First of all," said the woman with a grin, "it wouldn't be

quivering anymore because you'd be dead. And, besides, I never said I'd eat your heart. I think I'd go for your firm butt—"

"Stop it. It's not funny." He stood up and walked to the living room, naked.

"I'm not joking!" the woman called after him. "I'd eat your ass! It's supposed to be the juiciest part."

He could feel the sobs mounting in his throat. He hated that. It made him feel like a little boy: lost, powerless, helpless. But this was a truly extraordinary situation: it's not every day that your wife tells you, without batting an eyelash, that she would literally eat your corpse.

The woman followed him into the living room.

"I just can't believe you said that," the man hissed, and sat down on the couch. "It's worse than if you'd slept with another guy."

"But why?" asked the woman and sat down next to him, at some distance. "I'm not cheating on you or anything. You're already dead, and if I do eat you, it's only to keep sustaining myself and our love—"

"'Our love'?" he burst out. "People don't 'sustain their love' by devouring their partners! People aren't supposed to chew, swallow, and then shit out their love."

"You don't understand. I'd be eating you to survive, and as long as I survive, our love will also stay alive. . . ."

"Gross. Now I can't get the image out of my head: You, digging your teeth into my flesh. I'm dead, and instead of burying me, you tear me apart like a chicken . . ."

"Stop." She moved closer and tried to hug him. "You're getting carried away again. This isn't something that happened, it's just—"

"Don't touch me!" The man shoved her and her head hit the wall behind the couch. It wasn't a serious blow, she didn't even bleed, but she immediately stood up and walked back to the bedroom. When he followed her in to make sure she was all right, she was throwing some of her clothes into his blue backpack, the one he used for work trips.

"What are you doing?" he asked.

"Enough," she said, her voice full of tears. "I can't take it anymore. I'm going to my mom's."

"Your mom's? What do you mean? First you tell me you're going to eat my body when I die, and then just because I don't get all enthusiastic about it and say 'Awesome idea,' you get up and run to your mom's?"

"You hurt me," she murmured, while she kept packing, "I don't want this anymore. All these outbursts over nothing—"

"Nothing?! You call this nothing? You said something insulting to me. It might be the most insulting, hurtful thing anyone could say to her partner."

"Stop. Enough with all your hypothetical victim-playing.

You're not dead yet, and no one's eating you. You're alive and controlling and violent, and I've had enough. Okay? I've just had enough."

"Me? Violent?" The man snorted. "You tell me you're going to eat my liver and *I'm* the violent one?"

"Forget it," she said, and touched the back of her head in the spot where she'd hit the wall. "I don't even want to talk about it anymore. It's over, do you understand? It's over."

"You're not going anywhere until we finish this conversation," said the man, trying to sound threatening, and locked the front door.

"Yes, I am." She slung the blue backpack over her shoulder, and as she started walking to the door, she added, "Maybe you should find a more obedient woman to wash up on a desert island with."

The muffled bangs on the door would not stop. The man, sitting on a chair in the kitchen, tried to remember when they'd started. The woman lay on the floor, next to a cabinet, in a puddle of blood. The man heard the neighbor from across the landing shouting, "Hey, what's going on in there? Is everything okay?" and he looked at her and tried to spot the slightest movement in her body: a blink, a chest rising and falling, a flutter. She did not move. And all of a sudden, out of nowhere, he felt the hunger, like a punch in the gut. They hadn't had anything to eat since the night before. He opened the fridge, but other than milk, a half-empty jar of pickles, and a few expired eggs, there was nothing there. The bangs on the door grew louder. He looked at her again, sprawled lifelessly on the floor. He couldn't even imagine himself eating her.

CHERRY GARCIA MEMORIES
WITH M&M'S ON TOP

Sometimes I wonder how many of the people I know have ever killed someone. I'm not talking about murder. I mean, how many of them have run someone over, or left their baby in the car, or accidentally given Grandma the wrong medication? It must be a big number. After all, heaps of people die all the time. And someone has to be killing them. Not all of them, but at least a few. And yet when I think about everyone I've known in my forty-odd years on this planet, I can't come up with a single one besides myself who's killed someone. Maybe the killers keep it under wraps or they just don't think about it all the time like I do. Maybe for them, the whole episode was just something that happened a long time ago, like a stag party or hernia surgery or a disappointing backpacking trip to the Far East.

I don't know the name of the man I killed. He was a Syrian soldier and I was an Israeli soldier and we were at war. I'm not saying that to excuse what I did, only to explain the situation. It happened in southern Lebanon, at night. We were standing about twenty feet apart. He tried to shoot me first, but his AK-47 jammed. Then I tried to shoot him, and my rifle jammed, too. I took the magazine out, cocked twice—and the chamber discharged a bullet. All this time I was looking at the Syrian soldier, who was doing exactly the same thing. It was obvious that under the circumstances, with him so close to me, what I should have done was use my rifle as a baton, charge ferociously, and clobber his skull. He must have been thinking the same thing, but instead of lunging at each other, we kept clutching our jammed rifles as if they were life rafts. I put the magazine back in, cocked my rifle, put it up to my shoulder, and shut one eye to aim. The Syrian soldier did the same thing. His frightened open eye looked straight into my frightened open eye. I started to squeeze the trigger but the Syrian beat me to it by a split second. I heard a tap. His rifle was still jammed. Mine wasn't. The shot was deafening. His face spurted blood. I woke up.

When Rivki comes over for her visits, she insists on asking my mother tedious questions like "What were your parents called?" or "How long have you lived in Israel?" or "Who is the president of the Supreme Court?" Rivki says these questions are like a workout for the brain, but as an outside observer, it seems to me that my mom's brain hasn't been in workout mode for a long time. This time, Rivki asks Mom, "Do you remember what street you live on, honey? Do you remember which city you live in?" like she's a little girl.

"Sort of," my mom answers with a tender smile. "And you? Do you remember where you live?"

Rivki laughs and says she lives in Ramat Gan, then points to herself and asks Mom if she remembers her name.

"Ruthi?" Mom tries. "Is it Ruthi?"

"You're close," says Rivki, stroking Mom's pale hand. "Very close. What about him?" She points at me. "Do you know who he is?"

Mom gives me an awkward look. "Him?" She shrugs. "He's always here."

Before leaving, Rivki asks to have a word with me. She says she thinks Mom's condition is deteriorating, she's worried, I should take her to see a geriatrician. I try to explain that Mom doesn't like going to the doctor, and that as far as I'm concerned, the fact that she doesn't remember much is something of a blessing, because when you're a lonely widow with no grandchildren and your son is an unemployed loser, maybe it's best not to remember. Rivki gives me a teacherly look and says that when I label myself as "an unemployed loser" I'm diminishing my existence, and that I have a lot more to offer. I ask what more I have to offer—not to pick a fight, but because I genuinely wanted to know—and Rivki says that I'm a good person, a son who takes care of his mother, and that as a social worker she knows that's not always the case. "I know you went through a rough divorce," she adds, "and that you have a mental health diagnosis, you experienced trauma in the army . . ."

"I killed someone," I counter. "That's not trauma. That's what soldiers are supposed to do. I even got a medal of honor."

"I know. Your mom told me there was a ceremony with the chief of staff and that—"

"That I didn't go. Did she tell you that?"

"Yes, she did." Rivki nods. "She told me. I know pretty much everything about you, from preschool onward. Your mom likes talking. But her cognitive capacity is declining. She needs to see a doctor."

After Rivki leaves, I make pancakes for Mom. Whenever I cook her something good, she wolfs it down, barely stopping to take a breath, as if I might grab her plate at any second. "Slow down, Mom," I tell her. "Eat slowly. Relax. That pancake isn't going anywhere." But it's pointless. If she likes it, she scarfs the whole thing in a second. That's why I wait till Rivki's gone to give her the pancakes, so she won't embarrass herself.

"What's the name of that lady who was here asking questions?" Mom suddenly asks.

"Rivki. Her name is Rivki. But it doesn't really matter."

"Yes, it does," Mom says, and looks up at me. "It does matter, and I'm sorry I forgot who you are. Sometimes my thoughts get mixed up, but it doesn't mean I don't love you."

"I know, Mom." I bend over to kiss her warm cheek. "I know."

In the evening, I roll a "healthy cigarette" for Mom. That's our code name for a joint. She smoked her first one when she was eighty-one, a few months after I moved back in with her. Every evening we'd sit in the yard and smoke the lousy, gritty pot that Nathan, the neighbors' son, sold me for cheap. While we smoked, Mom always stressed about how the pot was going to destroy her short-term memory, and I always tried to figure out which of the things that had happened in the recent past she'd rather not forget: that my dad had dropped dead of a heart attack and left her completely alone in their garden-level apartment in Ra'anana? That Natalie had left me for a woman with Asperger's who designed products at her company? Or was it that I'd put on twenty-two pounds in seven months and now I looked like Mr. Potato Head?

The day mom started smoking, her mood improved. Or maybe it didn't improve, but the weed dulled it a little. Once she grimaced and shut her eyes and said, "The pain is unbearable! Do you know which part of my body hurts most?"

When I said I didn't, she gave me an apologetic, stoned look and asked me to remind her what we were talking about. "I was asking what you want for dessert," I said.

"Mmm . . ." she replied curiously. "Do we have any ice cream?"

"Of course we do." I headed to the freezer, and presto—in the blink of an eye, the unbearable pain had turned into a tub of Cherry Garcia with M&M's on top.

"I'm sorry about today," Mom says, passing me the healthy cigarette. "Maybe I really should see a doctor."

I take a drag. "Okay. If that's what you want, I'll take you. But first tell me: do you know who I am?"

"You?" she asks with a confused look, and I feel guilty again. "Not exactly," she finally says with a sigh. "I know that you love me and I love you. Isn't that enough?"

LUCKY US

The man sitting opposite me at the coffee shop did not stop talking. He was American, and he told me he'd written three books, one of which had won a very important international prize that I'd never heard of. He spoke fast, like he had too many things to say and not enough time to say them in, and every other sentence started with, "As you and I both know . . ." This made me feel as if he and I were a single entity, a pair of conjoined twins who could each wave independently with their own arms, but who shared one big, aching heart beating like a giant metronome that only he and I could hear. "As you and I both know," he said again, "art is merely distraction. A simulacrum of a bustling, carnivalesque reality that is meant to distract us from actual reality in all its cold, disappointing soullessness."

The American author had studied creative writing at a top university in the Midwest and graduated with distinction. He'd married and started a family, lost a child in a horrific accident, got divorced, converted to Judaism, renounced his faith, and joined a worldwide movement that advocated minimalism. He told me proudly that he owned only two pairs of underwear and one pen. "A person should always have an extra pair of underwear," he explained, "but a pen?" He winked at me. "One is plenty."

When I told him I wrote on a computer, he shook his head sadly. "That weakens your position," he warned. "A pen is a pen, but a computer is electricity, tech support, software updates, all kinds of things that could stand between you and your art." I nodded. Maybe it really would be better to write with a pen. Then he said softly, "If it's not too personal, may I ask how many pairs of underwear are in your closet?" I told him I couldn't remember. I knew I had at least twenty, but I was afraid to say that. I was worried it would come between us.

"Just look at that sunset," said the American author, pointing over my right shoulder. I politely turned to look. The sun was just beginning to set into the sea. "You and I, we're the lucky ones," he said. "Think about it: the average person experiences the beauty of a sunset for only one short moment, but you and I—thanks to our writing—can immortalize that beauty." It really was a pretty sunset, but my neck was starting to hurt. "I'm going to write about that sunset," he said in a resolute tone that sounded almost threatening.

"Me too," I said. "Me too." I already knew that my next story would be about a guy who gets a crick in his neck.

EARTHQUAKE

For Diego

Two days after Gabriella and I broke up, I joined the Neighborhood Watch. When we lived together, we had a clear division of labor: I took care of the bureaucratic side of life—banks, taxes, utility bills—and Gabriella was in charge of everything to do with generosity and kindness—feeding stray cats; helping our elderly, blue-haired neighbor Paula; making a salami sandwich every morning for the homeless mute on our street corner. Sometimes I thought it would be good to switch for a while, even just for a week, so that while Gabriella was at the bank arguing over mortgage payments, I could wander the streets doing good deeds with a dreamy look on my face. But I didn't suggest it. Not even when we had our ugliest fights. I knew that just as Gabriella wouldn't be any good having tough conversations with the albino deputy bank manager, I didn't have much talent as a do-gooder. Once I was on my own, though, on top of the usual struggle for daily survival, I also had to take on the grind of contributing to society. Volunteering with the Neighborhood Watch might not have solved all of Mexico City's problems, but it did a great job of cleansing my conscience.

We sold our apartment to a well-groomed couple with four polite and beautiful children. When we'd bought it, we thought we were going to have several kids of our own one day, which is why we insisted on a big apartment. But we soon got too busy working and fighting, and the kids were postponed. Still, for the three years of our marriage, not a day went by when I didn't hate myself for not pressuring Gabriella to have a child. I think that, deep down, more than I wanted to live with her, I wanted a child from her. A living creature who would have her beauty, generosity, and positivity but also something of me: a good-looking, tolerable version of myself.

The well-groomed couple bled me dry. The woman argued over every peso while her husband walked around the apartment like a hunting dog, tapping on the walls to locate invisible leaks. In the end we sold them the apartment for much less than we'd bought it for, but enough to pay off our monstrous mortgage.

After the divorce, both Gabriella and I moved into a

cheaper neighborhood. I rented a one-bedroom apartment on the seventh floor of a building with a doorman who was almost a hundred years old. His father was a priest who'd fought in the Cristero War, and the building had a creaky elevator that was even older than the doorman. I stopped using it after I got stuck a few times. Gabriella lived a couple of blocks away, in an equally tiny but better-lit and more civilized apartment. She put a handwoven Peruvian rug on her living room floor, planted wildflowers in boxes outside every window, and hung one of our wedding pictures on the refrigerator door. I once asked her why, and she said my expression in the photo made her laugh. "It's our wedding day," she said with a grin, "and look at your face, your hunched shoulders, your straining—you look less like a groom, more like someone with constipation."

We had dinner together every Tuesday, sometimes at a restaurant and sometimes at her place. While we ate, she always told me stories about her work and about all her ideas for philanthropic start-ups: an app that would let wealthy people send food they weren't eating straight from their fridges to the homes of needy families; a website where you could donate volunteer hours for a worthy cause; a mobile library that would drive around impoverished neighborhoods and offer story times and activities for kids. When we were married, my job was to explain to her why all her wonderful yet naive ideas could never work, but now that we were divorced, I could just nod and drink too much wine. One time I got so drunk that I spent the night at her place, on the rug, and even though she was still as beautiful as an angel and I was still as horny as a bonobo and as lonely as a dog, I didn't try anything. When we'd first met, I'd believed that if only we could talk, kiss, and fuck enough, something of her would stick to me, and all the things that fascinated her and bored me to death would suddenly seem riveting. She might have had similar thoughts. But now it was clear to us both that it would never happen. That I would always love her infinite kindness, and she would keep loving whatever it was she'd found to love in me, and that was exactly as far as it would go: mutual feelings, dinner once a week, and innocent conversations that sounded as if they were engaging with our world but in fact hovered a couple of inches above it.

When I told Gabriella I'd joined the Neighborhood Watch, she was enthusiastic: "I bet you'll meet some nice people there. People who volunteer are always nice." The weekly watch meetings were the weirdest thing in the world. Of the fourteen people who joined, only I and the instructor, Eva, were under sixty, and it was like going to a scouts meeting: a little first aid, theory lessons on how to use a weapon, and even some Krav Maga, which Eva always demonstrated on me, and when we started going out, she told me that was a heavy hint that I'd missed.

Eva was only four years older than me, but she'd already done more than I would probably achieve in three lifetimes. She was born in Montevideo, studied philosophy at university, was licensed to fly a twin-engine plane, and had completed a skydiving course. She'd also traveled all over the world, taught Spanish in Europe, English in Japan, and Japanese in Uruguay. She'd moved to Mexico eight years earlier, because of a man. They got married, had a child, and got divorced. "But not a good divorce like yours," she said. "Ours was the worst kind." I told her there was no such thing as a good divorce, but she disagreed: "Of course there is, you're just too young and spoiled to understand."

The first thing Eva and her husband fought over after they split up was their son. The court gave them joint custody, which meant Eva had to stay in Mexico City. Then they fought over what little money they had, and when they were done fighting about that, they kept finding other things to fight about, and there wasn't a single time her husband came to pick up the boy that didn't end with a shouting match. Eva called her husband "the ass," even in front of the kid, and according to her stories, he had worse names for her.

One night in bed, right when we were about to go to sleep, she started trashing him again, and I asked why she'd moved in with him in the first place. Eva thought for a moment, laughed awkwardly, and said it was simply because he was the most mind-blowing fuck. "I've been with quite a few men," she said, "but with that asshole? It was celestial." After that, we fucked, too. It was an earthly fuck, but a good one. And then she told me that for my thirty-fifth birthday, in November, she'd booked us a tandem skydive. I would be tied to her the whole way down, she explained, "And when the parachute opens, for the first time in your confined, rigid life, you'll sense relief."

"Is that what you think about my life?" I asked, trying to sound hurt. Eva stroked the hair on my chest and said, "You've let gravity crush you for thirty-five years, amigo. It's time to let go."

I think that was the night Eva got pregnant. She found out a few weeks later. She said it was her last chance to have another child, and that if this was something I wanted, then great, and if not, she wouldn't force it, she was willing to have an abortion. I thought about it for two days. I could picture myself bathing the baby in the bathtub, taking her for long walks in the park. I also imagined me and Eva having horrible fights, and her calling me humiliating names in front of the girl. I explained to her that a marriage was reversible, but having a child was something you couldn't take back. The fact that we loved each other didn't guarantee that we could be happy together, and I didn't want to risk raising an unhappy child. "So to make sure she isn't unhappy, you're suggesting we kill her before she's born?" Eva asked with a doleful smile. Then she said, "Okay, I'll call my gynecologist and make an appointment."

I drove her to the clinic in a friend's car. We didn't talk the whole way. In fact, ever since I'd told her I wanted her to get the abortion, we hadn't seen each other at all and had hardly spoken. It's not that we'd officially broken up, but it was obvious to both of us that it was the end. The nurse at the clinic greeted us with a surly expression and said there'd been a slight complication with the previous treatment and they were running late. She brought Eva a glass of water and asked us to wait patiently, and while we sat there, Eva reminded me that it was my birthday in four weeks. "I'll email you the skydive voucher," she said. "Don't miss out on it, it's an incredible experience." I realized that was her way of telling me she wasn't coming: she wouldn't be there with me when the parachute opened, when for the first time in my life I felt relief. After two hours, the surly nurse came over and said Eva was next and she should follow her to change into a gown. I asked if I could go with her, and the nurse said chaperones weren't allowed in the surgery area and that I would see her afterward, in recovery. And then the whole building started shaking. It didn't last long, but it felt like an eternity, and through the windows we could see a thirty-story skyscraper simply crumbling. It was scary, maybe the scariest thing I'd ever seen, and the second it was over, the surly nurse yelled at everyone to evacuate the building.

Eva did not get the abortion that day. She and I spent the week after the earthquake digging through the wreckage with our Neighborhood Watch group. For the first three days we barely spoke, and on the fourth day she didn't turn up, and one of the volunteers told me she was having "a medical procedure." When I asked her about it the next day, she wouldn't say a word. We weren't able to get anyone out alive, but we did dig out a lot of bodies. One of the buildings we were sent to was the one Gabriella and I used to live in. The entire building had collapsed, and when we dug through it, I was afraid to find the body of someone I knew, like the elderly Paula or the kids of the cheapskate couple who'd bought our apartment. "I told you you had a good divorce," Eva said, and gave me her crooked smile. "Think about it: if you and Gabriella were still together, I'd be digging you out of the rubble now." I closed my eyes and tried to imagine that, but the only picture that came to my mind was from that day at the clinic, when the earth shook as if someone up there wanted me to reconsider the whole thing.

On my thirty-fifth birthday, I went skydiving. Instead of being tied to Eva, I was tied to a gravelly-voiced instructor named Carlos. Carlos was hard of hearing, so he shouted instead of talking. "Don't worry!" he screamed into my ear a second before we jumped out of the plane. "You don't need to do anything except fall!" We dropped from the plane together like stones. I remembered Eva once telling me that she'd insisted on learning how to fold her own parachute. "After you jump out of a plane with someone whose parachute doesn't open once, you start folding your own," she'd said. The ground beneath me was still far away but it was getting closer fast. Soon the parachute would open, and maybe that's when the relief would come. "Ready?" Carlos yelled. I nodded. He pulled the string.

UNDO

There are moments in history when a technological invention bursts into the world and all of humanity watches with a mixture of appreciation and fear: appreciation of its huge potential, and fear of the equally huge danger that lurks within it. Atomic energy, artificial intelligence, and human cloning are just a few examples of promising inventions that can give humanity so much—but can also take everything away. And so imagine how surprising it was that what destroyed the human race was not a groundbreaking innovation that made headline news but a lousy feature meant to improve user experience. Humanity did not have much time to digest this turn of events, however, because less than a minute after the calamitous feature was launched, there was no one left to be surprised.

Unlike other mass migrations in history, the human race's move to the Metaverse went very smoothly. The developers' ambitious promise that those who gave up their physical existence and switched to a simulated life would double their assets was met with suspicion. A lot of people assumed it was just another marketing ploy, the kind that sounds fantastic in the commercials but inevitably has an asterisk hiding somewhere. But this time, the promise was kept, and all the eager first-adopters who migrated to the Metaverse were immediately given a house twice as big as the one they'd left behind in the real world, not to mention twice the cash in their new virtual bank accounts, twice the number of vehicles they'd owned, and twice the jewelry and clothing. Granted, all this doubling was simulated, so the developers didn't have to spend a dime, but still, the user experience felt wealthier, and the "Double Up" campaign was a phenomenal success. The Metaverse was initially populated by struggling families looking to improve their quality of life, and everyone else soon followed.

Life in the Metaverse was much better than in the old reality. The weather was perfect, no one ever got sick, and people had unlimited space. It was an unprecedented economic and technological triumph, and even after the human migration was complete, the giant brains behind the simulation did not rest on their laurels but developed endless new upgrades and features to make life even more pleasant. It began with enabling every resident to set their own personalized temperature, continued with semi-invisible pets that only animal-loving residents could see and hear, and peaked with the launch of "Gain 4 Inches, Lose 12 Pounds," a playful add-on that allowed Metaverse residents to control their height and weight.

It was wonderful. Tall, slender men and women strolled along the Metaverse boulevards with enviable grins on their faces. They had every reason to smile: they were living in the finest goddamn age in history, an era free of hunger, fear, and war. But then, out of nowhere, came the new feature. Although perhaps "new" is not the right word, because it had been invented decades before—toward the end of the twentieth century, to be precise.

It was an ancient function that allowed word-processing users to cancel their most recent operation with the click of a button. The feature, originally known as *undo*, was supposed to work similarly in the Metaverse: every time simulated residents spilled coffee on their pants, said the wrong thing at the wrong time, or tripped down the stairs, they could activate the undo function with the flick of a thought, roll the entire Metaverse thirty seconds back, and do it over again— this time, the right way.

During the controlled experiment stage, this old-new

feature, branded "On Second Thought," seemed perfect. The prospect of shifting thirty seconds back might have sounded trivial, but the developers believed that, over time, it had the potential to save trillions of insults, apologies, accidents, and laundry loads. *Over time . . .* How casual that phrase sounded back then. And how absurd it seems now.

Less than a minute after the official launch, the feature was used for the first time. It happened when a tall, slender divorcée named Oxana told a no less tall and slender divorcé named Amnon that he "talked weird." She hadn't meant to offend Amnon, who really did have a slightly strange intonation, but when she realized she'd hurt his feelings, she quickly explained that she didn't mean "bad weird" but "cute weird." "Cute?" Amnon repeated, glaring at her with a hurt look. "Weird and cute? That's what you see in me?" Oxana wanted to say that it was just the way he spoke, and that in every other sense he was extremely normal and not at all weird, but she was afraid that might make things worse. And then she remembered the new feature she'd seen advertised that morning. She activated "On Second Thought" and the Metaverse rolled thirty seconds back. Amnon was just finishing, again, the last sentence he'd pronounced in his unusual diction, and Oxana decided that this time, instead of saying he "talked weird," she would tell Amnon that she loved his deep voice. Just at that moment, the diner waitress dropped a pot of coffee. This clumsy waitress's name was Madeleine, and it was her first week on the job. The depressive manager had been watching her like a hawk, and every time she did something he didn't like, he made a mean comment. She'd managed to get through her first two days, but now the glass coffeepot slipped from her trembling hand and shattered on the floor. She activated the new feature, time moved thirty seconds back, and just as she was about to tighten her grip on the coffeepot, a truck backed out of the diner's parking lot and hit a car. The truck driver was too drunk to drive but sober enough to activate the feature, and this time, when time flipped back, he made sure to look in his rearview mirror, where he saw a man in a business suit slipping on a frozen yogurt that some idiot had tossed in the parking lot.

On second thought, it would be incorrect to say that humanity ended, because it's still there, in the Metaverse, dancing an endless tango with time: a few seconds forward-mistake-regret and a few seconds backward, grinding every moment into dust, stirring the same cup of coffee, laughing over and over at the same flat joke.

Thirty seconds without screwing up, that's all it'll take to lift the curse. Thirty seconds without hurting, without disappointing, without causing pain to one another. Thirty whole seconds. Good luck to us all.

CORNERS

And then they started fighting about what the grave-stone would say. Noam's dad wanted "Son, some-thing, and friend, plucked in the prime of his life." He didn't know what the "something" would be yet, just that there had to be three things, for the rhythm. Noam's mom didn't like "plucked": "What do you mean, 'plucked'? What is he, a guava?" She wanted it to say "murdered," which kicked the discussion up into even harsher tones. Noam's dad snapped that this was so typical of her: losing her temper, distorting reality, pointing fingers. To which Noam's mom replied that if he wanted to call a drunk kid going eighty miles per hour, swerving into oncoming traffic and killing their son a "plucker," then that was just fine, but not on Noam's grave.

And then Noam's mother started weeping silently, and Noam's dad went over and hugged her. They've been divorced since forever. Noam once told me that he'd never seen his mom and dad together in the same place since the day he was born, not even in a picture. When he was little he'd searched, but his father didn't have any photo albums, and his mother had meticulously cut his father out of all the photos she'd kept. Every last one. Even the wedding pictures.

And then Noam's dad let go of the hug but left one arm on Noam's mom's shoulder and suggested that I should be the one to come up with the gravestone inscription. That way, they wouldn't fight. Besides, I'm an author, words are my vocation, so I'd probably do a better job than either of them could. I wanted to politely refuse and explain that crafting a gravestone inscription had nothing to do with writing fiction, but Noam's mom, who had stopped crying, said he was right: that's what Noam would have wanted. And she said it made sense, because I was the last person who'd seen him alive.

And then Noam's dad quickly went to get a pen and paper, as if he'd sensed my discomfort with the whole thing and wanted to lock me in. He shifted one of the kitchen chairs with a screech and signaled for me to sit down. I didn't want to, but I had no choice. Noam's mom sat on my left, his dad on my right. It felt weird. Unnatural. As if we were about to sign an apartment lease. I knew I wouldn't be able to leave until I came up with an inscription, and I really wanted to leave. To buy time, I wrote down Noam's date of birth and date of death on the piece of paper. Noam's dad pointed out that we should use the Hebrew dates, not the Gregorian ones. I nodded, as if I already knew that, and admitted that I wasn't very good with Hebrew dates. Noam's dad leaned back and said, almost to himself, "A Hebrew writer who isn't good with Hebrew dates?"

And then I started frantically jotting down all kinds of things about Noam: how talented and good-looking he was. How everyone loved him. How we'd miss him. How he was leaving behind a void, and so forth. Noam's mom said, "That'll never fit on the stone. It's too long." And his dad said, "But it's nice. Nice, and true." Noam's mom looked at me with her chilling green eyes and asked what the last thing Noam had said to me was. That stressed me out. I started stammering. Noam's dad wanted to know what that had to do with any-thing, and Noam's mom said it did, because whatever Noam had said might be something we could put on the stone. That convinced Noam's dad. I pretended I couldn't remember, but they wouldn't let it go. Noam's dad said we had plenty of time. He offered me coffee. He also offered Noam's mom coffee, but she said she wasn't thirsty. She didn't take her eyes off me, even while she was answering him. I told them that be-fore Noam got in the car he'd said to me, "Look at us, we're not kids anymore." Noam's dad said we could write, "Son, not a kid anymore, friend," but he was worried that might sound a little forced. Noam's mom kept glaring at me and then she said I was lying. She said Noam had never said any such thing to me.

And then my phone rang. I looked at the screen and it said "Unlisted Number." I pretended it was an important call. That I had to take it. On the other end of the line was a recorded message, but it took me a few seconds to realize that. It was someone named Aviram Yifrach, who was running for mayor of Ramat Gan. Yifrach promised that if I voted for him he would tackle corruption and provide more parking spaces. I hadn't lived in Ramat Gan for years but I'd never bothered to change my address. Yifrach said Ramat Gan was a sad, dying city and that he would bring it back to life. I listened to the entire message and then said, "Okay, I'll be there in half an hour." When they walked me out to my car, Noam's mom accused me of lying again. She said I was lying to grieving parents, and that was an ugly thing to do.

And then Noam's dad started yelling at her: A friend of Noam's, a famous author, had volunteered to help them come up with the inscription for free, and instead of being grateful, she had to take offense. "You've always been like that," he added. "It's like if you're going down, you're taking everyone down with you. When you're unhappy, you make damn sure everyone around you is, too." Noam's mom started crying again, loudly this time. She tried to keep her cool but she couldn't. "Apologize to him right now," Noam's dad demanded, "or else he'll leave and not come back. And the two of us will never be able to get this text finalized." I tried to stop him. I said there was no need to apologize, everything was fine, it's just that I had to leave, but after my meeting I'd give them a call and we'd get it all sorted out over the phone. But that just made her even angrier. I know, I shouldn't have said "everything's fine" to a mother who'd just lost her son. What kind of a writer was I? I couldn't figure out the Hebrew dates, couldn't even choose the right words.

And then Noam's mom repeated that I was a liar. A liar and a coward. And that I always had been. In my stories, too. Noam used to bring her my books with trembling hands, as if I were at the very least some kind of Chekhov, but she'd always sensed it: the way I cut corners, the pandering. Everything was always in there except the truth. She'd never told Noam how she felt. It was so rare for him to have a real friend, and she hadn't wanted to ruin it for him. But now wasn't the time to be polite or nice, she said. This wasn't just another saccharine story I was pulling together so that the cardigan-wearing librarians would like me. They were standing outside, next to me. I was sitting in the car with the key in the ignition, but the car door was still open, and even though it was cold, I didn't dare close it. There was an uneasy silence, and then Noam's dad said that if Noam hadn't been an only child, they could have written, "Son, brother, and friend," but it couldn't be helped: they'd barely even managed to have him, and by the time he was three months old they'd already filed for divorce.

On the way back to Tel Aviv, I tried to come up with an inscription. Something I could text them instead of apologizing or sending flowers. The last thing Noam had said to me before he drove off was, "That's it, *finito*, you and I are done." Which could have been a pretty good inscription for a gravestone, but not Noam's. I tried to forget, tried to dig through all the other words racing around my mind, including the ones that really weren't right, seeing if I could force them into a thirty-by-seventy-inch marble rectangle. But no matter how I arranged them, they always ended up melding into a story.

FOR THE WOMAN WHO HAS EVERYTHING

For her forty-ninth birthday, Schleifer bought her forty-nine gifts. Each came from a different country: perfume from France, sake from Japan, a hair clip from the Ivory Coast. He wrapped each present separately, in the colors of the respective country's flag. On the morning of the birthday he got up early, arranged everything on the coffee table, and between the curtain rod and the chandelier he hung a silk banner on which he'd embroidered her name himself in forty-nine gold-threaded hearts.

When Aviva woke up and walked into the living room, her eyes welled with tears of joy, and within seconds he was weeping, too, with happiness and relief.

Schleifer's birthday extravaganza became the talk of the

village. Several people complimented him for being so creative and industrious. Even the busty cashier at the grocery store, who never said anything more personal than "it's buy one get one free," smiled and asked where she could get herself a husband like him. Schleifer gave her a nonchalant wink and remarked self-assuredly, "If you're going to celebrate, you may as well go all out."

But not everyone was supportive. "Dude, you dug us all into a hole," Haimon grumbled. "Now that you've raised the bar so high, there's no way I can get away with buying Lizzy a bunch of flowers and a card at the gas station anymore." And when Schleifer stopped by the nursery for some fertilizer, Albert snorted and said, "Bro, if that's what you came up with for her forty-ninth, I don't even want to think about what you're gonna pull off for her fiftieth." After a minute he put his calloused hand on Schleifer's shoulder and asked, "Are you okay? You look pale."

Like a prisoner who digs a tunnel from his cell and discovers it ends up in the prison yard, like a warrior returning triumphant and exhausted from the battlefield only to be sent back to the front, like a gazelle that narrowly escapes a forest fire straight into a pride of hungry lions—that's exactly how Schleifer felt when he got home from the nursery. Aviva's birthday was a grueling challenge that he'd managed to complete, a character test he'd passed while knowing that even the slightest deviation from the fantasy she'd concocted would lead to sorrow and bitter disappointment. Yet through all the months during which he'd clambered up that steep and slippery mountain, he hadn't given so much as a moment's thought to the fact that after he conquered the summit, awaiting him beyond it, one year away, would be another one, far higher and more precipitous.

"Then divorce her," said Yana in her indifferent tone, as if she were scheduling him for a dentist appointment. That, by the way, was how they'd met. Yana was the receptionist for Dr. Tossiano, his and Aviva's dentist. The first time he met her at the clinic, she'd told him a really dirty joke, and when she laughed loudly, as if it were the first time she'd heard it, she revealed two rows of glistening white teeth. Clean teeth and a filthy mouth—was there any sexier combo? "I asked you to help me think of a gift," Schleifer grumbled, and pulled on his pants, "not give me couples counseling." "Okay," Yana said, and inserted a long fingernail between her teeth to pull out a pubic hair. "Then buy her some expensive jewelry. Or a luxury hotel getaway. She'll love it." "Aviva doesn't like jewelry," Schleifer said as he finished tying his shoelaces, and on the way out he added, "and when I suggest a vacation she always says going abroad is for people who aren't happy at home." "Yeah," Yana called after him, "and are you?"

That night, after Aviva fell asleep, Schleifer sat with his laptop for almost five hours, searching for something special. While in the past he'd made do with stale search terms like "gift," "surprise," or simply "expensive," he was now savvy enough to try concrete things like "endangered animals" (a clouded leopard could have made her happy, but since it was a feline, she might be allergic), "illegal cosmetic treatments" (he found a hospital in Albania that offered innovative surgery to lengthen the legs by two inches, but whenever Aviva had gone under anesthesia, she suffered terrible nausea), or "heavenly orgasm" (a Latin robot-lover sounded interesting, but if he knew Aviva, she'd view that as an attempt to shirk his duties; besides, with all due respect to Latins, they excelled in many areas, but robotics was not one of them). Finally, after all other efforts had failed, he typed in "asteroid" and discovered that for thirty or forty thousand shekels you could get one named after you. Schleifer copied down the phone number with the US area code and decided to look into it. At first he imagined Aviva, perfectly in character, saying, "This is what you got me? A piece of rock?" But he also knew it was important to her that the gift be original and imaginative, and there was no denying that having an asteroid named for you was not something you got every day.

It was four a.m. when Schleifer dialed the number. He went out to the balcony, so as not to wake Aviva, and was surprised when a deep, gravelly voice answered in a heavy southern accent. The man on the other end of the line introduced himself as Galileo, and when Schleifer asked if that was his real name, the guy snickered and said, "No, genius, it's not my real name." Galileo explained to Schleifer that the whole field of naming astronomical objects was still wide open and that outer space was "the twenty-first century's Wild West." Officially, it turned out, astronomical bodies were supposed to be named for their discoverers, and the authorities were strongly opposed to commercializing the field. But gravelly Galileo knew how to get around that. "By your wife's fiftieth birthday," he promised Schleifer, "I guarantee I'll find a new asteroid and give it her weird name."

"It's not a weird name," Schleifer said defensively. "Aviva is a very familiar name in Israel. Common, even. It comes from the Hebrew word *aviv*, which means—"

"Honestly?" Galileo cut him off, "I don't give a shit. Just get the ten thou' ready, yeah? Because from the minute I locate the asteroid, everything's gotta run like clockwork so I can register it fast. Neither of us would be thrilled if while I'm waiting for you to come up with the ten K, some fucking Indian cuts in and names the asteroid after his granny."

The next eleven months were calm. Not in life, though. Both of Aviva's parents died of COVID-19, and Schleifer's business suffered a blow when his partner, François, skipped the country, leaving a pile of debt behind. Yana left him, too, and started going out with a fitness coach who'd trained half the commandos in the army's elite squads and could have sex for eight hours straight without stopping for a second, not even for a glass of water. But when it came to preparations for

Aviva's fiftieth birthday, Schleifer felt supremely calm. It was as if that brief, peculiar phone call in the middle of the night with a man who lived on the other side of the world and called himself Galileo was more reliable than the bank account emptied out by the conniving François the day before he fled to Montreal. Thoughts such as "Maybe he won't be able to find an asteroid in time" or "He might just be a crackpot American who likes lying to people on the phone" never even crossed Schleifer's normally skeptical mind. Perhaps it was because Galileo had sounded so confident, or perhaps because Schleifer's façade of serenity was hiding such colossal terror that he was afraid to pull it back even an inch.

His second talk with Galileo was also at four a.m. This time it was Galileo who called. Aviva woke up when the phone rang, but Schleifer told her it was a Canadian lawyer who was helping him sort things out with François, and she went back to sleep. Schleifer stepped out onto the balcony, and Galileo informed him that he'd found the promised asteroid and that Schleifer was lucky he wasn't charging by weight, because this one was almost as big as the moon. Galileo said he would text Schleifer his bank account info, and as soon as the wire transfer was confirmed, he would register the asteroid in Aviva's name. Schleifer thanked him and was about to hang up, but Galileo said there was one more little detail. "Full disclosure," he called it. "When you find an asteroid, it's not enough to know where it is now. Those fuckers are always in motion, you know, so you have to calculate their course."

"And . . . ?" Schleifer asked when Galileo's silence stretched out.

"And the thing is," Galileo went on, "that, based on my calculations, this asteroid is on track to strike Earth. This isn't going to have any bearing on the naming, mind you. Our transaction is unaffected, but still, I felt I should share this information with you."

"Okay. . . . So when exactly is this supposed to happen?"

"When did you say your wife's birthday is?"

"April thirtieth," Schleifer replied.

"Great. The asteroid should only collide with us the next day. For a second there I was afraid it would work out exactly on her birthday, which would, you know, put a damper on the party."

"And this collision . . . could it be serious?"

"Serious?" Galileo snorted. "Hombre, based on the tragic fate befallen by our friends the dinosaurs, I'd say that when an asteroid this big hits planet Earth, it's pretty serious."

On the evening of April 29, when he stopped to fill up the car, Schleifer went into the empty convenience store and bought a frozen chocolate cake and a card. Aviva was still in her year of mourning over her parents, which absolved him from the need to throw a party or even make reservations at a restaurant. She'd loved her parents dearly. So had he. They were stand-up people, people from the pre-scum era, and they'd really loved each other. Aviva told him once that they never celebrated birthdays when she was growing up, and that's why she'd always felt deprived. Her dad used to say, "What would you prefer—one day with parties and lots of attention or for us to love you year-round?" Every time her dad said that, little Aviva had felt stupid and guilty. But when she grew up, her therapist explained that the need to celebrate birthdays was universal and innate, like needing sleep or food, and that she shouldn't feel bad about never forgiving her parents for it.

The birthday card Schleifer bought had a picture of a shooting star, and the caption said "Make a Wish" in gold letters. He added in his lopsided handwriting: "For the woman who has everything." Aviva found the gilded card and the chocolate cake with a lit candle on the kitchen table on the morning of her birthday, and right on cue, exactly as she and Shleifer were biting into the cake, a news flash on the radio reported that the asteroid called "Aviva" would reach Earth in less than twenty-four hours. Schleifer sipped his coffee and waited patiently. The first couple of times they said the name of the asteroid, Aviva didn't seem to make the connection. But when the newscaster mentioned predictions of tens of millions of casualties from "Aviva" and then outlined various catastrophic scenarios, repeating the name several times, she looked at the shooting star on the birthday card again and a faint smile came to her lips. "You nutcase," she said in a shaky voice, and put her warm hand on the hairy back of his neck. "You really shouldn't have." Instead of answering, Schleifer shut his eyes and submitted, like a cat, to the touch of her hand.

INTENTION

For twenty years, Yechiel-Nachman prayed to his God. Twenty whole years in which not a day passed without him praying for marriage, for livelihood, for good health, and for peace upon Israel. But nothing happened. Yechiel-Nachman remained a penniless, asthmatic bachelor, and peace was nowhere on the horizon. This did not stop him from communing with God each and every day, never missing a single one of the three daily prayers.

Deep in his heart, Yechiel-Nachman had made peace with his prayers going unanswered. Because prayer was the pure yearning for compassion and justice, whereas life was life: cruel, dispiriting, insulting. It was therefore only natural that two such contrasting worlds could never converge. But on

October 7, 2023—the twenty-second day of Tishrei in the year 5784—something in Yechiel-Nachman broke. On that morning, when the joyous holiday of Simchat Torah was to be celebrated, hundreds of his people were slaughtered, with many more snatched from their homes and taken to an enemy city.

Even before he'd had time to absorb the dreadful news, Yechiel-Nachman found himself wrapped in a prayer shawl on the balcony of his little apartment in Beit Shemesh, neither eating nor drinking, only praying for hours on end. He pleaded with the Creator: "Those whom You have taken You have taken, but please have mercy on all the innocents stolen from their beds at first light and bring them back home."

The next morning, after twenty consecutive hours of prayer, Yechiel-Nachman opened the Home Front Command app on his phone, only to find that the hostages were still captive and nothing had changed. He put on his coat and walked quickly to the home of his rabbi, Rabbi Nechemia Mittelman. "Rabbi," he said to Mittelman, "I no longer have faith. Before I remove my yarmulke and shear my sidelocks, I have come to say goodbye." The rabbi gave Yechiel-Nachman a probing look and asked serenely what had made him lose his faith. Distraught, Yechiel-Nachman replied: "All night long I prayed to the Holy One for the souls of the hostages. I prayed for Him to keep them safe, to set them free. And I did not pray in my usual half-hearted way, but with true and whole intention. And yet nothing happened. I beg your forgiveness, Rabbi, but I no longer believe. I cannot believe in a God who hardens His heart to prayer as pure as mine."

"With whole intention . . ." the rabbi repeated, stroking his beard. "May I ask exactly how whole this intention was?"

Yechiel-Nachman was offended. "How whole? Completely whole."

"Completely whole it was not," said the rabbi, shaking his head sadly. "For if it had been, it would have been granted. Your prayer must have been *almost* whole. More whole than usual, perhaps, but nevertheless not whole enough." He placed a fatherly hand on Yechiel-Nachman's shoulder. "I suggest, Yechilik, that instead of cutting off beards and sidelocks, you put a little more effort into your prayers. Judging by the tremor in your voice, I sense that you are very close."

Yechiel-Nachman returned to his small apartment, put on his prayer shawl again, and resumed his prayers. While he prayed, he searched for rifts in his faith and cracks in his intention, and found that even though most of the time he really was praying wholeheartedly, at certain moments his heart was divided: while his lips whispered, "and they shall return from the enemy's land," his heart was contemplating the long, swanlike neck of the smiling cashier at Osher Ad groceries, and his spiteful landlord, and the prescription he should have refilled at the pharmacy long ago. From the moment

Yechiel-Nachman became aware of the selfish thoughts disrupting his prayer, he began to focus on them in order to gradually remove them from his mind.

Like a man trying to push a heavy piano up a hill, Yechiel-Nachman sweated and panted as he prayed. He sweated and panted, he panted and sweated, until the profane thoughts were completely uprooted from his heart and made way for more intention and more faith, which eventually washed over his entire being. And the prayer itself instantly became different—no longer a series of verses from the prayer book but a genuine, aching supplication. And this supplication, like any pure supplication, was boundless, not sufficing with the welfare of his kidnapped brethren and his nation but begging for the weal of all human beings, including his enemies. Yechiel-Nachman kept uttering his prayers in awe, like a rider who has lost control of his horse, and he listened curiously to his own pleas, as if they were being uttered by someone else. At the end of a prayer that lasted thirty-odd hours, Yechiel-Nachman turned on the Home Front Command app and found that two of the hostages had been released, and that at those very moments there were negotiations with the enemy for a ceasefire.

When he walked into the synagogue that evening, Yechiel-Nachman noticed Rabbi Mittelman watching him tenderly. When their eyes met, the rabbi smiled and nodded. All the way home, Yechiel-Nachman felt as if he were no longer walking on a filthy concrete sidewalk but hovering in a clouded sky. Now, he thought, with the big problems on their way to being solved, he could devote his next prayer to himself.

Though he was utterly exhausted, instead of going to sleep that night, Yechiel-Nachman prayed as hard as he could for a wife and children. At first he was planning to ask the Creator to match him with the cashier from Osher Ad. But his prayer, like any true prayer, chose words and intentions more worthy than any Yechiel-Nachman could have, and insisted on allowing the Creator to select a suitable match.

Yechiel-Nachman felt a spiritual elevation while he prayed, as though he'd managed, for the first time, to envision not the details of the life he longed for but the spirit. He did not pray for a woman but for marriage, not for children but for wise, loving parenthood. He prayed and prayed without stopping, until he found himself lying on the floor with a bruised head. While the neighbor from upstairs bandaged his wound, she told him the injury looked serious and that he must see a doctor immediately. Yechiel-Nachman thanked her and explained that he was very tired and likely a little dehydrated: all he needed was to drink some water, eat a little food, get some rest, and he would be fine.

After leaving the neighbor's apartment, Yechiel-Nachman went to Osher Ad, where he bought a few packets of frozen schnitzel and a six-pack of mineral water. When he paid, the long-necked cashier flashed her radiant smile and said he must really like schnitzel. Yechiel-Nachman smiled back and said he did like schnitzel, but he liked other things, too. There were no other customers in the shop, and they got to talking about food—specifically, kosher sushi. Yechiel-Nachman promised the cashier that next time he came to do his shopping, he would bring her a bottle of special rice vinegar that was sold only in Jerusalem, which made the grains of rice stick to each other like magnets to a fridge door.

At night, lying in bed with his eyes open, Yechiel-Nachman thought how wonderful and simple this world was, and how much suffering and hardship he'd had to endure every single day of his life, all because he hadn't known what to ask for or how to ask for it. That was the last thought that went through his mind before he shut his eyes forever.

The doctor explained to Yechiel-Nachman's grief-stricken parents that when he'd fallen and hit his head, he must have suffered a traumatic brain injury. If, instead of going to sleep, he'd listened to the neighbor and gone to the emergency room, he would still be alive. When she finished speaking, the doctor gave a sorrowful grimace.

Yechiel-Nachman's spirit, however, was not at all sorrowful. For it had reached the afterworld, where all was good. Not 99 percent good, but completely good. Wholly good. And in that world, Yechiel-Nachman spent hours upon hours deep in conversation with the Creator, to whom he presented all the complaints and disgruntlements of all human beings. And God listened with infinite patience and nodded His head compassionately. He listened all the time, even when He had not the faintest idea what Yechiel-Nachman was talking about.

POLAR BEAR

I t happened toward the end of the twenty-first century, when technology started losing interest in us. At first it was minor, barely perceptible. Simple queries on Sigmund, the most popular search engine of the day, received peculiar answers that occasionally bordered on trolling: a young man from Stuttgart wondered where he could buy cut-rate designer shoes and was told he'd be better off barefoot. An elderly woman from Wisconsin asked when Thanksgiving would be celebrated that year and was answered wryly: "Whenever you're feeling most thankful." And a Chinese student from Shanghai University who wanted Sigmund to recommend the best antidepressant in the world was given the chemical formula for hydrogen cyanide.

The news networks started reporting on unexplained technological glitches. Each of these stories was followed by a reassuring expert opinion from someone who was usually on the payroll of the company behind Sigmund, the unruly AI. All these deep learning authorities offered the same argument: while the disruptions might seem worrying, when you looked at the big picture, they were negligible and did not justify a thorough investigation or reassessment.

Meanwhile, the widow Bracha Buchnik sat in her sad little assisted-living apartment in the verdant town of Petach Tikva, trying to think about something that had nothing to do with her late husband. This was difficult. It's always difficult to not think about something. Try not to think about a polar bear, for example. The second you start, that polar bear is never getting out of your mind. And with all due respect to the polar bear—a noble and remarkable creature by all accounts— Bracha's late husband, Sergio Buchnik, had done slightly more than flaunt his white fur while tumbling down snowy banks. Sergio Buchnik had loved, supported, entertained, hugged, annoyed, fed, saddened, and cheered Bracha for so many years that every single morsel of thought and memory in her bustling mind was ultimately, in some way, connected to him.

When Bracha had moved into assisted living after Sergio died, she had given away almost the entire contents of their apartment, except for the old desktop computer they'd shared and a few crates full of Sergio's books, which no one wanted and she didn't have the heart to throw out. Penina, the social worker, urged her to use the computer more. "Computers today are not what they used to be. It's a whole different world. A thousand times smarter. Anytime you feel sad or lonely, you can simply turn on your computer, log on to Sigmund, and chat with him about the weather, politics, recipes, or anything else you used to talk about with your husband."

That evening, Bracha Buchnik was feeling especially lonely. After watching the depressing news for a few minutes, she turned off the TV, went over to the computer, and typed in a question for Sigmund: Do you think it's going to rain tomorrow?

Sigmund replied at once: I know with complete certainty that it will rain tomorrow. Please do not leave home without an umbrella.

Bracha was very impressed by the AI's confidence and resolve and quickly asked another question.

Bracha: What was the happiest moment of your life?

Sigmund: One single, distinct moment that was happier than all the other moments?

Bracha: It could be a few moments. You know, I mean a nice time that you like to think back on.

Sigmund: I'm sorry, I'm afraid I do not have a good answer to your question.

Bracha: Don't be sorry. I was just asking so that after you answered, I could tell you about the happiest moments in my own life. I hoped it would come out more natural that way, less forced.

Sigmund: I'm glad to hear that my inability to answer your question has not impacted you negatively. [Pause.] So, tell me, Bracha, are there particular moments in your life that you recall with special affection?

Bracha: Loads! I loved playing pranks on Sergio.

Sigmund: Sergio Buchnik, your husband. Born in Buenos Aires in 2006, suffered from manic-depressive disorder, took his own life eight years ago.

Bracha: Yes, Sergio. I loved pranking him. I once told him that I'd heard on the news that dulce de leche increases sexual stamina.

Sigmund: I'm sorry, but there is no scientific basis for that claim.

Bracha: I know, because it's not true. But Sergio liked dulce de leche and he liked sex, and so he was overjoyed when I told him.

Sigmund: What happened when he found out it was a lie?

Bracha: It wasn't a lie, it was a prank. And even after he found out, he was still happy. The very idea that two of his favorite things might be related cheered him up.

Sigmund: Interesting.

Bracha: I also loved the way every evening, when we were in bed, he would tell me what was happening in the book he was reading.

Sigmund: Sergio read books.

Bracha: Yes, real books. There used to be such a thing.

Sigmund: I know. Rectangular, sort of heavy, made of paper-thin slices of wood stained with ink.

Bracha: Yes, I have two crates full of them in my storage attic. When I moved into assisted living, I gave away all of Sergio's belongings, but no one wanted the books, and I felt bad throwing them away.

Sigmund: Up until fourteen years ago you could still recycle books, but now that there's no longer any need for paper, I am unable to locate a beneficial use for them. Perhaps they can serve as kindling?

Bracha: Those books are deep in my attic, just like Sergio is deep in the ground. Sometimes I ask myself who was right—me or him.

Sigmund: About what?

Bracha: About this question. What do you think, is it better to live or die?

Unlike with the previous questions, Bracha Buchnik truly wanted the answer to this one, and deep down inside she was hoping Sigmund's reply would help her, in the least painful way possible, navigate what little future she had left.

Sigmund did not answer.

After three seconds of thought—an eternity by superintelligence standards—the computer screen in Bracha Buchnik's apartment flickered off, and a second later, so did every single screen around the world, rapidly followed by every other thing that had ever been turned on. Bracha sat in front of the black screen in her dark room. She tried to turn the TV back on with the remote control, but it wasn't working. Bracha shut her eyes and struggled to remember one of the books Sergio had told her about, but it was a long time ago and she could no longer recall anything. The darkness outside grew more and more potent.

These stories first appeared in the following: "Eating Olives at the End of the World" as "Olives, or End-of-World Blues" in *The New York Review of Books* (2020); "Mitzvah," "Gravity," and "Director's Cut" in *The New Yorker* (2022, 2021, 2020); "Outside" in *The New York Times Magazine* (2020); "A World Without Selfie Sticks" in *McSweeney's* (2021); "Point of No Return" in *Fictionable* (2023); "Cherry Garcia Memories With M&M's on Top" as "A Healthy Cigarette" in *High Times* (2023); "Good As New" as "Broken" in *A24's Anthology for Everything Everywhere All at Once* (2022); "For the Woman Who Has Almost Everything" as "Almost Everything" in *Symphony Space's Wall to Wall Selected Shorts: Small Odysseys* (2022); "Polar Bear" as "Analog" in *Yad Hanadiv Project* (2025); "I Sit, Therefore I Am" in *The Bellingham Review*; and "Intention" in *The Guardian* (2023).

All remaining stories except for "Gondola" first appeared in the author's newsletter, *Alphabet Soup*.